LITTLE

NYMPH

LITTLE NYMPH

ELIZABETH STEVENS WRITING AS

E.J. KNOX

Kinky Siren
an imprint of Sleeping Dragon Books

Little Nymph
by E.J. Knox

Paperback ISBN: 978-1925928457
Digital ISBN: 978-1925928440

Cover art by: Izzie Duffield

Copyright 2023 Elizabeth Stevens

Worldwide Electronic & Digital Rights
Worldwide English Language Print Rights

CONTENTS

AUTHOR'S NOTE

This is a dark, angsty, contemporary new adult bully/enemies-to-lovers, mafia romance with enough steam to melt your screen. Do not engage in public consumption unless your poker face is impenetrable. Do not read if you don't like alpha males claiming what's theirs, a feisty heroine with a secret past, complicated love triangles, excellent side characters, forbidden romances full of passion and dirty words, or serious cliff-hangers (I am so sorry!).

This story will continue in *Little Secret* and conclude in *Little Truths*, and will go on to feature the heroine in sexual situations with two love interests. While not considered cheating by the characters, you may have different feelings. Proceed with caution.

I kept the origins of Echo and Olive vague for reasons, but they have a lot of Australian in them, which may explain a lot. 99% of the dialogue that feels clunky will be that way on purpose. Either because the speaker is not a native of English, or because they talk like an Australian. Apologies if you hate it.

This book is written using Australian English. This will affect the spelling, grammar and syntax you may be used to. It might come across as typos, awkward sentences, poor grammar, or missed/wrong words. In the majority of cases (I won't claim it's infallible, despite all best efforts), this is intentional and just an Aussie way of speaking (it took my US beta readers a bit to get used to). I can't say 'the' Aussie way, since we seem to differ even within the same state. Just think of us as a weird mix of British and US vernacular and colloquialisms, but with our own randomness thrown in. I still hope you enjoy it, though!

CHAPTER ONE

I felt Olive take my hand and pulled my eyes off the scenery to look at her. She was still staring out her window, but I saw her chewing her lip the way she did when she was nervous or worried.

"I'm still here," I assured her. "I will *always* be here."

She nodded. "Are you sure about this, Echo? I feel like it's a lot to ask."

I smiled. Looking back out my own window, I squeezed her hand.

God love my best friend. I certainly did.

Even if I wasn't sure – which I was – it was a bit late to back out now. Like a car, plane, second plane, boat, then second car trip too late to back out now.

"This has been the plan for years, Ollie," I reminded her. "I love you and there is no way you're going without me."

Olive wouldn't survive without me. Her dad's words but, as much as I loved Olive like we'd shared a womb, he was right. She was sweet and kind, and it was in her to trust everyone and only see the good in them. It was her very nature and, by the time she was twelve and her mum was gone, her dad hadn't had the heart to nurture it out of her.

I vividly remembered the day he stopped trying.

Olive with golden ribbons in her dark brown hair, her white dress flaring as she span in the sunlight on the lawn of their estate. She was smiling and laughing, her grasping less than me the news her father had delivered to us earlier that day. Oh, he'd known it for goddamn years, and he'd tried to prepare her, but he'd only just told us.

He'd put his hand on my shoulder as we watched her dance in the sunshine. I'd felt him squeeze it gently and knew he was worried about something. I'd put my hand on his and looked up at him.

"She'll need you, Echo," Daniel had said, taking a deep breath. "She'll need you by her side."

I remember being confused at his words, knowing there was no world in which I wouldn't be by Olive's side. I'd been by her side for nine years, and living as a sister to her for the last three. I didn't remember a time we weren't together.

"Is this about this morning?" I'd asked.

He'd nodded. "I can't prepare her properly without destroying her light."

I'd squeezed his hand back, knowing what he was saying and why. "It's okay," I'd reassured him. "That's what she has me for."

"You are far too young to know what you might be giving up," he'd replied sadly.

I'd shaken my head. "I would give up everything for her."

"Echo…" Daniel's voice did just that in my mind until, "Echo?" in Olive's small voice pulled me back to the present and I shook my head.

Turning back to her, I saw she was looking at me with those gorgeous big blue eyes that had all the boys back home falling over themselves for her.

"I'm not going anywhere, Ollie."

I reached over the seat and hugged her. It took a moment, but she finally relaxed in my arms and hugged me back.

Yeah. Where we were going, she was going to need me. I'd spent the six years since her dad's bombshell doing everything to protect her light. Most days, I knew the only light left in me came from her, but that was a fine price to pay for everything she and her father had given me after my mother succumbed to her demons. Of course, Mum hadn't done that until she'd passed a fair few of them on to me.

I felt the car slow and Corvi said, "The Vitali property, ladies," as I gently pulled away from Olive.

As I looked out the window to the guard booth beside the big stone and wrought iron gates, I knew Olive would be adjusting her dress and smoothing her soft curls. She always looked good, and it was annoyingly effortless on her part.

"You ready?" I asked her.

"Ready." Her tone was chipper and optimistic. "I'm sure it'll be fine."

I smiled. "Sure. What's spending the summer with the guy you're expected to marry but never met?"

"The whole point of the summer is to get to know him before it's official."

I nodded as we pulled up to the front door. "No. 'Course. Let's pretend you have a choice in the matter."

"Echo…" she said softly, her chastising full of love.

I nodded as I clocked Corvi getting out of the front passenger seat. As Olive's designated bodyguard, he'd been with us since we left home, and he'd be with us until – if – we went home again.

"I know. I know," I sighed. "Play nice."

She smiled demurely at me as someone not-Corvi in a suit opened her door. Not even Corvi was coming for Little Old Me's door, so I put my hand out to open it. Then it was pulled out of my reach. Suddenly, I was staring into piercing grey-green eyes and my stomach bottomed out.

While my brain was trying to restart and I was trying to remember how to breathe, I watched the eyes narrow on me. He leant one hand on the open door, and the other, heavily tattooed arm on the car body as he ran his tongue over his teeth. And it did nothing to help me remember my own name.

My eyes scanned him quickly, drinking him in like he was water the morning after a *really* big night.

Tailored black suit trousers. Equally tailored shirt, sleeves rolled up, and maybe three buttons undone, hinting at a body's worth of tatts I wanted to explore. Preferably with my tongue. There was a smattering of dark stubble over his jaw, and I got distracted from anything else about him as I watched him lick his bottom lip.

"You're not Miss Carlione," he said, pronouncing Olive's surname with the classic accented twist.

Jesus. No voice had ever had that effect on me. Literal goosebumps. Tingles. Tight nipples. Be still my beating clit. All of that.

"What exactly gave it away?" I asked cheekily.

Something flickered deep in his eyes. I didn't catch precisely what it was, but I liked it. I really liked it.

A whole summer in this place was suddenly looking far more interesting. While Olive was busy being wooed by her prince captor, maybe I could be doing a little wooing of my own.

My mystery guy looked me over again and there was a definite spark of heat in his eyes. I tried to play it cool and not show just how much he was affecting me. Then his mouth puckered slightly, and he pushed off the car to look at Olive. Which left me looking straight into his crotch.

Not that I minded.

But I did curse the lack of x-ray vision.

"Miss Carlione?" he said smoothly.

"Yes?" Olive answered, sounding like she was surprised anyone was looking for her.

I looked up and saw mystery guy incline his head. "Welcome to my father's home."

Well, fuck.

But there was still a chance my new insta-lust wasn't the end of the world.

However, when his smug eyes darted almost imperceptibly down to me as though to say, 'Oh, yeah. Enjoy the view? By the way, I'm your best friend's future husband,' there was no mistaking which Vitali had opened my door.

Motherfucker…

Of course, any guy who could practically stop my heart by just existing would be utterly out of reach to someone like me.

Mikhail fucking Vitali.

Better known as Maverick. Stupid name, but I got it. Who wanted to be named after the guy who killed their grandfather as a way for their father to remember the vendetta? I mean that's a pretty fucking easy thing to remember. Isn't it?

And I'd spent six years hearing *all* about him.

About the whole Vitali family.

I knew who the Vitalis were even before Daniel had spent hours with me most nights for the last four years, locked in his study after Olive had gone to bed, going over files. Teaching me the ins and outs. Preparing me to fight – literally and figuratively – the battles that Olive couldn't fight herself. He'd been hesitant in the beginning, but I'd worn him down. Personally, I believed he was glad I had because it got us what we both wanted; Olive, happy and protected.

"Are you waiting on an invitation there, Miss Sumpter?" another voice pulled me out of my own head, and I looked up again to see another generic suited thug.

"That'd be just swell," I told Thug Two as I unfolded myself from the car.

Unfolded here being simply the action required to get out of the awkward position I'd put myself. I was a short arse. Because all good stories revolved around a plucky short girl just trying to keep her and her loved ones sane.

Thug Two looked me over like he wasn't sure who or what I was. As he turned his head to the front door, eyes always scanning everything, I saw an earpiece.

These Vitali's weren't fucking around.

But then, I didn't expect any less. Daniel's men – and women – including Corvi, wore earpieces as well. All the better for coordination and prior warning. Not that it had done my mum much good. Accidents sill happened.

I looked towards the front door and saw Maverick leading Olive up the steps. She snuck a look back to me and I gave her a slight nod. She pressed her lips into a tight smile and nodded back.

"If you'll follow me, Miss Sumpter," Thug Two said.

I didn't bother asking him what would happen then. Now that Olive and I were there, we were at the whim of Lord Vitali and his household. I'd prepared for that to be our lives. If I followed the thug, I'd find out whatever he clearly didn't think it necessary to tell me was coming next.

I indicated he lead the way and then dutifully followed him up the stairs and through the front door.

If the outside wasn't enough to know that the Vitalis were dripping in money, the inside sure gave it away.

The place was like this medieval, renovated castle, covered in vines and sitting atop a hill. Surrounding us were vineyards and rolling hills and just gorgeous country I was itching to explore. Lots of laneways and valleys to get lost in while Olive and Maverick were 'getting to know each other' and I was little more than a spare wheel.

The entry hall soared above our heads, and I was just crude enough to do a full three-sixty-degree spin to take it all in. Wood panelling and stone. Glided – or solid – decorations everywhere. Sweeping staircase – of course. And actual suits of armour. I had to stifle an excited squeak. It was only achieved by shoving my fist in my mouth.

Thug Two showed me towards a door. I just caught sight of someone else going through it and hoped it was Maverick and Olive. Thinking it probably better to hide the more acerbic elements of my nature as long as possible, I went the way the thug pointed without question or sassy commentary, and my patience was – for once – rewarded.

"...lovelier than your pictures, Olive," Enrico Vitali was saying to her, because that man could only be Maverick's father.

Slightly shorter than his son, but still clearly in his prime, they could have been the same person at different stages of their life. With one exception. Enrico's eyes were deep brown.

Okay, two exceptions.

Enrico was smiling and relaxed. Maverick looked like there was a goddamn stick up his arse as he surveyed the room. But then I was distracted.

A very attractive young man beelined straight for me as soon as I settled into the room. I mean, he had nothing on the arsehole that was Maverick Vitali, but he was still a good-looking guy.

Sun-kissed olive skin, with cropped, caramel hair. Bright, light brown eyes. A five o'clock shadow, at best. And some very fine bone structure. He was dressed similarly to Maverick, but in dark grey. And, had I been inclined to get him naked, I expected some very impressive muscles hid under that suit.

He held a hand to me, and I gave him mine. He pressed a lingering kiss to the back of it, as those cheeky eyes looked up at me.

"Miss Sumpter," he said and, quite frankly, his voice was also very lovely. "Antonio Calabrese. I believe we've both been called to chaperone duty."

Yeah, all right, Antonio. I see you. Cheeky bugger. I felt like we might get along quite well. He was certainly, on first impressions, much more amiable than Maverick.

I smirked. "So, you pulled the short straw, too, Mr Calabrese."

He gave me an answering smirk that made his eyes twinkle mischievously. "Antonio, please."

"Then, you'll call me Echo, Antonio."

He inclined his head. "Echo."

"Tino," Maverick barked.

"The boss calls," he said with a knowing wink, before pressing one more kiss to the back of my hand and sauntering to said boss, whose eyes were so fixed on me I was worried they might put a hole in me.

I stood on the fringes of the group. Watching Lord Vitali butter Olive up and peacock over his castle and son. Olive all decorous and genteel as she smiled, kept her eyes down, and nodded politely. Maverick deep in intense conversation with Antonio. Conversation being a polite description of what looked more like Maverick barking orders at my, for lack of a better word, colleague.

I'd always been on the outer edges and, once I'd been introduced to Lord Vitali and made a prompt break back to the fringes, I took the opportunity to slink out. I caught Corvi's eye on the way out and I saw the warning in it.

He wouldn't stop me doing anything. He knew he couldn't. We'd played that game before, and both been damned lucky no harm came to Olive. He also knew I could take care of myself. In this kind of setting anyway. We were Lord Vitali's guests. How much damage could we come to?

Across the entry hall, I caught sight of myself in an unnecessarily large mirror and could see exactly why Maverick had known I wasn't Olive. She was tall and willowy and classically beautiful, with her dark brown hair and big, innocent blue eyes. She was always in pastels and soft things. Dresses. Blouses. Even her jeans, the rare occasion she wore them, seemed soft and proper. After the hours of travel, she still looked like she'd just stepped out of the bathroom.

Then, there was me. Dirty blonde hair with shadow roots designed to hide my regrowth as long as possible, pulled back in a messy ponytail. Smudged eyeliner because I insisted on wearing too much like I belonged in the early 2000s. Too many curves, or so said the woman who took over as Olive's governess after Mum was committed. My jeans were acid washed, dark, ripped. My sneakers were scuffed. My dark purple tee slouched off my shoulder, exposing the black singlet strap failing to cover my bra strap.

We were chalk and cheese, Olive and I. Total opposites. And yet, I loved her more than anything else in the world.

I stuck my hands in my pockets as I set off to wander. I was used to these sorts of houses. Daniel had a few. And the kitchens – and therefore, the staff – were usually in a certain direction. The signs were there if you knew what you were looking for.

"Miss Sumpter?" someone very servile-looking guessed, and I nodded. "Can I help you?"

I shook my head. "Just on my way to the kitchen," I told her.

She nodded. "Let us know if you need anything."

"Thanks."

I found my way into the kitchen and looked around.

"Help you, miss?" someone asked.

I shook my head. "Just getting the lay of the land. I'm Echo. Sumpter. I'm here with Miss Carlione."

"Is she as pretty in real life?" another asked and got whacked for their trouble.

I laughed. "Prettier. And nicer."

I'd always got on well with the staff, being a daughter of one myself. With one foot in both worlds, I gravitated down the pecking order rather than up. I was the kind of girl who preferred to be on guard than guarded. I wanted the anonymity to make ALL the stupid choices, and not have them blasted across the news or gossip rags. I wasn't socialite or peer material, and I was quite happy about that.

A guy wiped his hands on his apron and held one out to me. "Dom," he said. "I'm in charge when Saracco's upstairs."

"Sarraco's the butler?"

Dom nodded. "*Maggiordomo.*"

I nodded as well. "*Maggiordomo,*" I repeated, getting my mouth around the word. Then blinked. "Oh, like majordomo."

"Exactly as."

I grinned. "Awesome."

Dom introduced me to some of the others and gave me all the highlights about where they hung out on their off nights. I always liked to know where the servants hung out. That's where I'd find kind of guys I preferred to love and leave. I lost track of time as I chatted with them, finding more occasion to laugh or smile than I expected I'd get that whole summer. And they teased me mercilessly about my accent. Or lack thereof.

Finally, one of Vitali's thugs said, "Best get yourself to dinner, Miss Sumpter," as they entered the kitchen.

I sighed and nodded to the staff as I pushed away from the bench and slid off the stool I'd found myself on. "Remember me with fondness," I said loftily.

Dom smiled. "You are welcome any time, miss."

I followed the thug back to the dining room. Enrico, Antonio and Olive were seated already. As well as a young woman and man I hadn't met yet. I gave them all a terse smile as I took my seat next to

Olive.

"Slumming it with the staff again?" she teased, and I snorted in an effort not to burst into laughter.

The smile was still at my lips as movement made me look up to see who had the misfortune of sitting across from me.

As Maverick took his seat, his eyes never left my face. There was a look in them I couldn't identify. Olive coughed in her tell-tale 'hiding a laugh' kind of way and I had to bite my lip to stop myself laughing as well.

Maverick's eyes dropped to my lips and everything in me fluttered. Just before I dropped my eyes, his rose to them again, and I froze.

I told myself nothing zinged between us, but I wasn't sure how much I believed me.

"Now. Echo," Enrico Vitali said, and my gaze snapped to him. "You disappeared before we had the chance to talk."

"I like to get acquainted with a place," I told him. "Makes it easier to plan our escape."

Something twinkled deep in Enrico's eyes as they flitted to his son and back. "Indeed. I am told you met Mikhail and Antonio. However, you missed meeting my other children. Adriana is my firstborn. And my youngest, Vincenzo."

Which explained the other two at the table. I looked to them both as he indicated them and nodded as pleasantly as my hesitance to meet new people allowed.

"Adriana's husband will be joining us next week," Enrico continued.

Adriana looked at her father before saying to me, "He had to work."

She was all dark hair and eyes, and stunningly gorgeous. But then, I was inclined to think of everyone as beautiful. Olive called it a credit and a strength. I tended to think of it as a woefully neglected libido.

"Tell me more about you," Enrico said to me firmly. It wasn't a request.

I shot a side-look to Olive. "Well, Mr Vitali–"

"Rico, please."

Oh. That was a power play and no mistake. I inclined my head to show him I heard loud and clear.

"Well, *Rico*. There's not much to tell. My mum was Olive's governess. When she…fell ill, I was lucky enough to be taken on as Daniel's ward."

"And your role here?" Rico asked, as though he didn't know. "What do you expect to get out of this summer?"

Okay. We were playing that game? I could play that game.

"I'm here to make sure *no one*," I paused pointedly, "takes advantage of Olive. Us women need strength in numbers, Rico. Any authority we *might* have tends to be taken by you men."

The corner of Rico's lips twitched like he was fighting a smile. Then his eyebrows jumped as he sat back in his chair. "Is that so?"

I nodded.

Sure, I'd planned on hiding my more acerbic qualities. At least for a few days. But the proverbial cat was out of the equally proverbial bag now and there was no way it was going back in.

"It is. Olive might be nice and polite, but you'll find I lack her tact, *Rico*."

Rico huffed a laugh. "Yin and yang, no?"

I nodded. "Yin and yang."

Rico's amused grin widened. "Daniel warned me about you, Echo. I told him he had to be exaggerating. I see now he was not." He thumped the table and Olive jumped. "Good. Then wherever Olive goes, you go, too. *Lo equilibrio*. Balance. Yes?"

Clearly, I was supposed to answer. Not that I had a choice in what my answer was.

"Yes," I said evenly.

"Good." he laughed. "Good. Now, wine!"

As the staff poured wine, I felt Olive's eyes on me. I snuck a look at her and saw the amused exasperation shining in them.

"*Viva!*" Rico cheered and the others followed suit.

I nodded resignedly as I picked up my wine. "*Viva*," I muttered, with slightly less enthusiasm as anyone else.

CHAPTER TWO

"Think of it like royal families," Daniel had told me once.

"Royal families?" I'd asked and he'd nodded.

"Our marriages are pacts. Deals. More money. More status. More power. More whatever we want or need."

"So, what does Ollie marrying Vitali's son get you?"

He'd sighed. "Protection."

"From?"

"The Vitalis."

"They're shaking you down with a marriage contract? Why?" I paused as I thought about it. "They didn't know how beautiful she'd be. How smart. How kind. What do they want her for?"

Daniel had hesitated for a moment and, when he spoke, wouldn't meet my eyes. "She gives them legitimacy in our circles. A legitimacy they don't have to take by force. Fear gets them so far; they also need respect which fear alone doesn't get them."

"I don't like it," I'd told him then and I still didn't like it.

I didn't like that my best friend was walking to an arranged marriage. What made it worse was that she'd never once fought it. Because that's who she was. She was a people pleaser. A pushover. Did whatever was asked of her the way she'd been brought up. She was also kind and lovely and just wanted to make other people happy, so I couldn't entirely fault her. I just wished she'd make some tiny rebellion. But then, that would appease *me*. Knowing her the way I did; she was doing what she needed to do to get through it. Or, the thought had literally not even occurred to her that she could. Either could be equally true.

So, no. She wouldn't say a word against the Vitalis or her father, or their plans for her. But she *would* fully rip into my outfit choice the next morning after coming into my room to wake me up.

"No," Olive said as I walked out of the bathroom. She shook her head. "No. You can't wear that."

I looked down at myself. Pale jeans shorts and a white singlet, paired with flat sandals. It was weather appropriate. It was comfortable. I looked available but not *scandalously* available; classy yet relaxed. It should have ticked all the boxes.

"Why not?" I asked.

"We're not travelling now, Coco. You need to look…"

"Like you?" I suggested.

"The part," was her resigned acknowledgement.

I sighed, knowing it was futile to argue. "Fine! Fine. I'll change."

Sparing her grateful smile a more sarcastic one in return, I stomped into my wardrobe and looked at my meagre offerings. My stuff looked pathetic, taking up barely an eighth of the size of the wardrobe itself.

The last six years, I'd expected to be in the background. Not front and centre. By Olive's side hadn't literally meant *at* her side, but Rico had been clear the night before that I'd go quite literally wherever Olive went. I could argue, but I was under no delusions that Olive would bear the brunt of any punishment my disobedience would incur.

I breathed out heavily. "I'm going to need to do some shopping," I muttered.

"Daddy has been going on about making you put more on your card," Olive sang enticingly from the door.

I gave her a nod in acknowledgement, but nothing else.

Daniel had given me a card on his credit account, same as Olive, when I turned fifteen. It was an allowance of sorts, just there was no limit. I could put whatever I wanted on it, and I was expected to use it to perpetuate the image of my status as Daniel's ward. And now as Olive's chaperone, I guessed.

Obviously, I barely used the card and, when I did, I certainly wasn't shopping at the boutiques where everything was so expensive it didn't even have price tags. It wasn't my style. Give me cheapo grunge online webstores any day.

I should have known that this trip called for designer boutiques with no price tags.

"Convenient that this place has a hundred of them, then," I said to myself.

"What?" Olive asked absently.

I shook my head. "What are your plans for today? I could go down to the village and get some shopping done?"

I chose not to dress *like that*. It wasn't for lack of grasping the concept or knowing exactly how it was done.

"If you think you're going shopping without me, you're wrong. And there's nothing planned until afternoon tea, so we've got time."

I looked at her hopefully. "So, I can out go like this."

All hope was dashed. "Cream trousers and black satin cami."

Because, of course, she knew my wardrobe better than I did.

I groaned. "But I have to wear *the shoes* with the cream trousers."

She nodded. "Exactly."

"They might kill me."

"I might kill you."

"And yet, the shoes are scarier."

"And yet, you rock them so hard."

I snorted. "Look at you trying to be all punk."

She flicked her hair. "We do your stuff sometimes."

I nodded. "That we do. Okay, cream trousers. But," I looked at her pointedly, "we're doing brunch in the village and Corvi's not invited *and* I'm having too many mimosas."

She shrugged. "We're on holiday. Just drink the champagne straight."

I looked at her, pride overflowing. "Eighteen looks good on you."

She inclined her head. "I like being legal."

I laughed. "Okay. Good. Cream trousers. Monster murder heels. And black satin cami."

When I was dressed, we weren't allowed to leave until she'd fussed over my hair, putting a more definite curl in my blonde waves and yet somehow not making us look like day/night clones. But finally, we were heading downstairs to meet Corvi and the car out front.

The monster wedges made me as tall as Olive, and I did feel fucking fabulous. Not that I'd ever tell her that.

Corvi drove us down to the village. The topography was so hilly that the road wound lazily across the hills, up and down, and it took us three times longer to get down to the village than it would have otherwise. But it gave us a chance to put the top down on the Rolls Royce Dawn that Rico had shipped over just for Olive to use. She'd had her choice of colour and I'd helped her talk Rico out of hot purple for a slightly less obnoxious deep turquoise.

Olive put a scarf on both our heads, and I felt like I was in *Roman Holiday* or, knowing my luck and personality, more like starring in my own version of *Bridget Jones*.

The village was appropriately busy. Bustling enough for a summer holiday destination, but with few enough people driving that we found a park easily. Convenient.

Olive and I linked arms and strode down the street, popping into a couple of shops for the hell of it, before finding a place that took our fancy for brunch.

As we sat on a sofa and looked over the Mediterranean sea, made our way through a bottle of Champagne and waited for our food, we did boring things like talk about how nice the weather was – although, it was actually really nice – and our rooms, and how comfortable our beds were and how we slept the night before.

Finally, talk got around to more interesting things.

"What do you think of your boy toy so far?" I asked her.

She spluttered a tipsy laugh. "No spark." She shook her head. "I think I had more spark with every nun back at school."

I smiled at that imagery. "Well, that sucks."

She shrugged. "Maybe we'll get engaged, get married, become friends, then eventually fall in love."

"I like the order you put that in," I pointed out and she giggled. Olive after a couple of drinks had always been so much more relaxed than any other Olive I knew.

"Look," she said. "Maybe we can have live-in lovers, and all the kids can be conceived by IVF?"

We looked at each other, tying to keep our composure, but both failed. A bubble of laughter burst out of us at the same time. Olive slid her arm through mine and leant her head to me.

"There are worse ways to live."

"No. No. I agree. I'm just surprised you've put that much thought into it."

"It was a long trip. And you snore," she accused.

I smiled and hugged her arm. "Only when you drag me a million hours from home."

"Please," she laughed. "If I'd left you home, you'd have followed me in ten minutes."

How easy it was to dismiss her trepidation from our first arrival now that we were two girls strolling under the Mediterranean sunshine with all the visage of freedom, even if Corvi had both eyes on us and would be with us in seconds if we needed it. Not that we would, because the whole island was arse deep in Vitali loyalty. We were, supposedly, the safest we would ever be anywhere.

Not that she was wrong.

Miss out on three months, in summer, on a gorgeous, secluded island where I would be the most free I'd ever been in my whole life? Miss out on a luxurious vacation with my absolute best friend in the world? Sunbathing and rambling through the countryside? Perving on stunning, muscular men in the tightest of bathers?

No freaking way.

Even the shopping was fun.

But then, shopping on holiday didn't count, did it?

Every shop assistant seemed to know who we were. We were fawned over. We were plied with actual Champagne, not just delicious bubbles. And, Jesus, did we shop.

Enough dresses and pants and shorts and tops to convince Olive that I would look the part for every breakfast, lunch, dinner or made-up meal I was dragged to.

A ball gown I was never going to wear.

Make that three.

And a bunch of glitzy, glamourous, shiny things to wear clubbing. Of the drinking and dancing type. Not the baby seal type.

Now that we were of age, and on an island filled with men I was hopefully never going to see again, I planned to make full use of the numerous nightclubs. Having only been to one nightclub and feeling woefully underdressed, I wasn't going to risk being caught out again.

"Echo Sumpter!" Olive cried as I walked out of the change room.

"Knock out?" I teased, striking a pose.

"K.O." Olive nodded, in her feeble imitation of the Tekken voice over, as she fell back into the couch.

As we walked out of the store, we bumped – not quite literally – into Maverick and Antonio.

"Shopping?" Antonio asked happily.

Olive nodded. "Coco's wardrobe was found a little wanting. We're putting that to rights."

"She is lucky she has someone to show her propriety," Maverick said mock-caringly.

I took a step towards Maverick with a fierce, "Oh, I'll show you–" but Olive hissed an, "Echo!" at me while shooting him a saccharin smile, and I stopped.

Maverick smirked knowingly at me, a challenge. A shit-stirring cheek I wanted to slap right off his face.

"Something you want to say to me, *Mikhail*?" I asked him, snidely.

The smirk fell. "My father might find you amusing, *mezza sega*. But I am less lenient than him."

I didn't doubt it for a second. Maverick screamed tightly wound, harsh punisher with a significant lack of knowledge or experience of the concept of fun or shenanigans. I mean, I wouldn't mind finding out if he was just as domineering in the bedroom, but that was a sure-fire way to complicate things if ever there was one.

Maverick inclined his head to Olive, threw me a look of utter hatred, and swept away. Antonio gave me a knowing smirk and a wink, and followed after him.

"Oh my God, Coco," Olive sighed when they were out of ear shot. "You promised Daddy that you'd behave."

I frowned at Maverick's retreating backside, even if I was simultaneously wondering if it was tight enough to bounce my hand off.

So, the rest of the week *was* me behaving.

I continued to dress the part. Which involved even more shopping, much to my annoyance. But the time spent relatively alone, pretending we weren't leading her to veritable slaughter, with Olive was awesome.

On Friday, there was a cocktail party, and it was the first time I didn't wear pants or a jumpsuit. I actually wore a dress. One that brushed peskily just above my knees. Only because Olive threatened to smack me if I didn't.

It wasn't until I walked out onto the patio of the Vitali palazzo, blowing a stray hair resignedly from my face, that I realised it was the first time I'd had any leg on show since we arrived. Unusual for me, but still true.

"Stop fidgeting," Olive hissed. "You look amazing."

"Is it too short? Should I have worn a bra?"

She schooled her smile to aim a warm greeting to Rico across the patio. "It's refined, and no. Unlike some of us, you've got enough to hold it up without help."

I snorted, completely undignified, as I tugged on the strap of my dress. "I still can't believe I'm not spilling out of it. This like never happens."

"All the more reason that dress was fate," Olive said.

"Yeah, not a big believer in fate, Ollie."

"Well, considering it's put more emotion on Maverick's face than I've seen all week, you might want to start believing."

My eyes panned until I found him at the opposite end of the patio to his father, and his eyes were fixed on me. Or, more accurately, my legs, like he'd been living with mermaids his whole life and never seen a single leg in his whole existence. I just couldn't tell if the scowl on his face and surprise in his eyes was because he liked it or because he hated it.

"He looks like he just threw up a little in his mouth," I told her, which is how I knew he wasn't looking at her. No one had ever thrown up a little in their mouths because they looked at Olive.

"Maybe the bruschetta disagreed with him?"

I looked at her, glaringly, as I picked up a beer from a passing waiter's tray.

Olive extricated it from my hand and exchanged it for a fancy looking rosé, and picked one up for herself as well. She gave the waiter a nod, then turned back to me with the wine.

"I'm not you, Ollie," I reminded her as I took it.

"No, you're my yang, I hear," she said as I took a sip.

I snorted wine up the back of my nose. "So, why am I in a dress, and why don't I get the beer?"

"Because there's enough yang in you already."

"Shame there isn't more *wang* in me," I muttered as Maverick and Antonio walked over to us. "Antonio, hi," I said loudly to cover for Olive's sudden, inexplicable spluttering.

He smiled as though he was interested in the joke, but wouldn't dare ask. "Good evening, ladies. You look lovely, Echo," he said, and I inclined my head in thanks.

Because it would be improper for him to comment on Olive's appearance. That was Maverick's job. Not that he was concerned about the particulars of his job description just then.

My eyes darted unconsciously to Maverick. His eyes were firmly pointed at my cleavage, of which there was ample on display, I'd admit. There was a heat deep in them that stoked the embers in me, but I stamped them down furiously. Insta-lust was one thing. Continuing to lust after my best friend's intended when I knew full well who he was was another.

Not that said lust was easy to ignore.

Both of them looked stunning in their dinner jackets and shirts. Antonio was in a blue jacket with white shirt and pale chinos, while Maverick was in all black as seemed his favourite colour-scheme. But I would be the last one to tell him to quit it, because it did everything for him. The only turn off was that neither of them had socks on – or, visible socks at least – and there was something about that I'd never been able to get behind. I got it spoke to a certain style, but it made me think of sweaty feet and…

Actually, that was just what I needed to dampen my lust for Maverick.

Picturing him with sweaty feet. Ew. Brilliant. Good job, me.

"…canapes are never enough at these things, don't you agree?" Antonio was asking, and it seemed like both Maverick and I were pulled out of our own heads at the same time.

Maverick cleared his throat as he finally looked at Olive. Not that she appeared to mind he'd quite obviously had his eyes attached to my chest for the past I-didn't-want-to-know-how-many minutes.

"Miss Carlione," he said, his voice low and deep and making my body do things it was decidedly not supposed to do.

From the corner of my eye, I saw another waiter heading our way. So, I drained my glass and swapped it out for another, which didn't last long either.

I floated around the party behind Olive, taking my 'everywhere she goes' orders very literally as she was introduced to everyone, and Rico told everyone how lovely and beautiful she was, and what a perfect daughter-in-law she was going to make.

But only physically.

Mentally, I was following Maverick around the party.

I couldn't keep my damned eyes off him. And for no other reason than maybe he liked the look of me in this dress and definitely I liked the look of him in that suit. It was an horrendously shallow and ridiculous reason, but I had an overactive imagination that just wouldn't let me get the idea that I'd affected him out of my head.

Not for the first time, I wished that Olive saw anything in him, because I'd do a far better job at not lusting after a guy my best friend wasn't just expected to marry but also actually liked.

Luck was not on my side, and I looked for every opportunity to slink away. It was a long time coming, but I finally found it.

So it was, a little before midnight, that I was out by the garage with a few of the staff having a rare but well-deserved smoke in my finery. The party was still in full swing judging by the noise from the patio, but we heard heavy steps crunching on the gravel as we laughed.

"Evening, sir," one of them said and I looked up.

Maverick Vitali himself was coming along to the garage, swinging his keys around his finger. He'd swapped his dinner jacket for a leather one and clearly mussed up his hair. I hadn't seen him with his hair like that before. So rugged and more natural. It suited him. It suited me. The whole package suited me, and I'd had too many drinks not to totally perve on it.

Maverick gave the group at large a nod. The warm, smoky smile on my lips was fading just as those eyes alighted on me. Something came over him as he realised it was me and not another servant. For good measure, I took another slow drag.

"Inside," Maverick snarled to the rest of them.

At least, when I turned to go, he softly wrapped his hand around my wrist, confirming my theory that he'd been dismissing everyone *but* me.

"Not you, Miss Sumpter."

"Something wrong?" I sassed him.

"What are you doing?"

"Enjoying my gilded prison for the first time this week." Little bit of an exaggeration, but oh well. "What are you doing? Sneaking out of Daddy's party to do just the same?"

I looked down to where he still had hold of my wrist. It was the one still holding the cigarette. His hand trailed down almost like he was going to take my hand, but instead deftly took the cigarette from me and took a drag himself before crushing it under his massive boot.

"So, you are the good girl who likes to play at dirty." It was a question that he didn't want or need me to answer.

I grinned as I bit my lip. "You'll find there's very little *good* about me, Mikhail."

His face twitched, but I didn't know why.

He stepped towards me, forcing my back against the wall, and didn't stop until he was close enough for me to feel the edge of his jacket brushing my stomach. It sent a mad dash of butterflies chasing through it.

"What do you want me to say, Miss Sumpter?" he purred, like he knew we'd entered a dance and he was stepping up to the challenge. "That I am the bad boy who wants to play at good?"

I was drunk and that was my only – piss poor – defence for flirting with him not once, but twice.

"For Olive's sake, I hope that's true..." I left the end of the sentence hanging wildly and hoped he'd rise to the bait.

He did, as he searched my eyes for something. "But not yours?"

I shook my head slowly and felt my body lean into him. My brain vaguely registered a reminder he was off-limits and a total jerk, but I refused to heed it.

I leant my lips up to his ear, needing to steady myself with a hand on his tight, warm chest. "I've always had a thing for the wrong guys."

Maverick pressed into me, and I want to say I didn't melt against him. But I did. And I was sure he was very aware of that. Mainly because, it felt like maybe he melted against me as well.

His lips dropped to my ear, and he rumbled, "Funny, I've never had a thing for the right girl before."

My heart fluttered wildly as he just pulled away and continued sauntering wherever it was Maverick Vitali sauntered off to in the middle of the night. I was frozen in place, my head stuttering and having no idea what to think or say or do.

The next thing I knew, a motorbike was roaring to life and sped past me on its way to the gate.

"Oh, no, you didn't," I whispered, far too late and to nobody in particular.

Maverick Vitali might be the death of me. But, boy, it'd be a pretty good way to go.

CHAPTER THREE

"Okay, Mr Wall. It's you and me," I said as I rubbed my hands together.

Never had I been so happy that I'd packed my hiking boots for this trip. The most I'd been brave enough to Google about the Vitalis was this damned island and, as soon as I'd seen the vistas, I'd known there was no way I wasn't getting out in it as much as possible.

Which made this, as my first foray into said gorgeous countryside in over a week of being there, exceedingly laughable.

I'd got myself completely lost, with my phone lying snug on my bed back at the manor. My only bearing was the occasional roar of an engine which I logically knew meant a road, so I was making my way there in the hope someone would come along and be able to get me back to the Vitalis in one piece.

Except now there was this wall standing between me and my goal. It was a quaint little rock thing that stood about as high as my arm pit. It stretched on for a million miles in both directions and I was worried that, if I tried to find an easier crossing point, I'd lose what remained of said – useless – bearings.

I was sure I'd seen in a movie or something that walls like this took master builders to make, that there was some secret to making them so well. I mean, that was all well and good, but it didn't help me get over it.

"Okay. Climbing. I'm not averse to climbing. I climb all the time. If I was still fourteen." I breathed out heavily. "No. Easy."

With another car zipping along the road that I was sure was getting closer, I took another deep huff and launched myself at the wall. Instantly, I felt the rock gouge into my knee and down my shin as my foot scrabbled for purchase. Not that it was all that comfortable on my hands or stomach either.

"Shit," I grunted, trying to ignore the sting as I hauled myself to the top. "I remember this being easier..."

Once there, I took a second to look around. It was goddamn breathtaking. Just over the wall was a thicket – I think they were called thickets – of bushes or hedge or whatever. Regardless of what it was, I'd still have to scramble my way through. But what was a few badges of honour for my jaunt through the wilderness?

I could see a road winding back and forth over the hills, a car now and then driving along. There was currently a car coming towards me, and I figured this was my shot. I waved my arms – a little too enthusiastically – and took a dive off the top of the wall. As I tried to catch my fall, I heard car brakes screeching but landed awkwardly on my ankle and got a little distracted.

Then a car door slammed, and I felt a rush of relief. Whoever had been passing had obviously stopped and got out. Hopefully because they'd seen me rather than a coincidental need to pee.

"Thank you," I muttered to no one in particular, and I tried to stand. "ARGH!" I cried out painfully, feeling tears prick my eyes, as I dropped back to the ground.

It was far too loud for the feeling that burst in my ankle but overreacting to pain had always been my strong suit.

The bushes between me and the road rustled like something large and dangerous was running towards me. My heart thudded. Relief was replaced with a very hesitant dread.

I scrambled back until the rocks of the wall dug into my back and waited to be eaten alive by whatever giant beastie was coming for me.

A figure burst out of the bushes and I gasped, "Shit!" as I recognised them and held my hand to my rapidly beating heart. "What are you trying to do? Give a girl a heart attack?" I snapped.

Maverick pulled himself up and I realised he had a fresh cut on his cheek and another on his arm. Had I not known him better, I'd have thought he'd run hell for leather through those bushes for me without a single second thought for himself.

He was wearing tight black jeans, black boots and a black tee that clung to his muscles. I wanted to say he didn't look good. But he always looked good. He looked damn lickable as he stood there, looming over me. I had some very impure thoughts about what could happen next, despite the thunderous look on his face.

He was breathing heavily as he glared utter fury at me. "What in the fuck are you doing? You could have fallen off a cliff!"

I shrugged wildly and in annoyance. "Who builds a wall on a cliff?" I yelled.

"Everyone!" he yelled back. "How else to stop idiots falling to their death?" The word 'idiots' was accompanied by a vague gesture in my direction.

I narrowed my eyes at him. "I'm sure you'd prefer this idiot *had* fallen to their death."

"Yes, I ran up this hill, through fucking branches, hoping to find your mangled body at the bottom of a cliff because it would be easier for *me*," he huffed.

"You don't need to sound so pleased about the idea," I muttered.

He snarled. "Get up. I'll take you back."

He made to walk away, then stopped when he realised I was still sitting on the ground.

"Get up, Miss Sumpter," he barked.

I cleared my throat and tucked my hair behind my ear as I looked away from him. "I'm fine. I'll find my own way back."

"You think I'm going to take advantage of you?"

A thrill ran through me that I furiously stamped down. "I'll be fine," I repeated.

Even had I been able to stand, I didn't want to be stuck in a car with him for more time than it was necessary to get back because of the stupid twisty turny roads. Not that I wanted to tell him either of those things.

"Get. The. Fuck. Up," he growled.

I shifted on the ground and cleared my throat again. "I'll see you back there."

He stomped over to me and grabbed my arm. It was rough, but he didn't hurt me. As he pulled me up, I put too much weight on my twisted ankle and grunted as I fell against him.

"What's wrong?" he asked.

"You almost sound like you care," I huffed as I pushed him away.

He didn't let go of me, but helped me back to the ground carefully, squatting beside me, those thick thighs straining against his jeans. "Your ankle?" he asked, and I reluctantly nodded. "Let me see."

"I'll be fine. I just have to rest it for a minute. Do whatever you're doing, and I'll see you for dinner."

"You will not make it back in time for dinner."

I shrugged, ignoring his words as true in the face of the sun kissing the distant hills. "Okay. Order me a late supper, then. I'll have it when I get there."

"If you can't walk, I will carry you." He made to pick me up and I batted him away. "Now is not the time for your disobedience, Miss Sumpter," he growled and my whole body felt it then promptly pretended it didn't

"You're not carrying me," I said, pushing him away further.

He fell on his arse, mouthed something I doubted was complimentary, then rearranged to sit beside me.

"What are you doing?" I asked him.

He dragged his thumb over the corner of his mouth and threw me an unimpressed sideways glance. "We stay until you can walk. Then I drive you back."

I blinked. "You don't have to wait. I'll be fine."

He licked his bottom lip, looking like he was about to just pick me up regardless of consent. Finally, he said, "At least, let me look at it."

I huffed a laugh. "And what are you going to do about it?"

He growled in annoyance, and I thought he was getting up, but he just shifted to in front of my feet. "Which ankle?" he snapped, and I saw in his eyes that he was nearing the end of his tether with me.

I swallowed my sassy retort. "Right." I pointed somewhat unnecessarily at it.

He bowed his head as he started undoing my shoelace. For a guy who didn't go anywhere without storming or racing or shouldering or shoving, he was incredibly gentle. He got my shoe and sock off with minor pain and even an almost imperceptible, 'forgive me,' at my two winces of discomfort.

With my ankle free from its confines, I saw it looked fine, just a little red. Maverick ran his fingers slowly over it in a manner that could really only rightly be called a caress. The beginning teases of tingles wound from his fingers up my leg, and I was glad he was looking at my foot so he didn't see me lick my lip and have to force a deeper breath. Very gently, he checked my range of motion and the functionality of the rest of my foot.

Then his hand followed those tingles, as they flared to bright and beautiful life deep in my pelvis, up my leg to check the gash under my knee. His fingers trailed around behind my knee and his hand cupped my upper calf. His other hand brushed a little higher up my leg presumably under the guise of making sure that was the extent of my injuries when he finally looked up at me through his eyelashes and my traitorous heat goddamn stopped.

I had to force another breath and realised that I was holding myself rigid. It had less to do with me wishing he wasn't touching me, and more to do with my concern about what my body would try doing if I didn't have total control over it.

Heat was heavy in his eyes, and I couldn't keep my breathing from being too shallow. I couldn't stop my tongue darting out to lick my lip again, and I knew I wanted it to be his. In the space of a single heartbeat, I imagined exactly what he could to do me right there. And no one would ever know.

Him leaning forward, pulling me roughly by my hips to let him nestle between my legs as he kissed me deeply. His hands hot on my waist, sliding in between my shorts and singlet. Hands tightening. Gripping me firmly. The force of it telling me that he wanted me – that he hated me – as much as I wanted – hated – him.

I felt his hand slide further up my leg and dragged myself back to reality to find a humoured smirk in his eyes, and the hint of a matching smirk at his lips.

"Didn't anyone ever tell you to wear appropriate clothes for a hike, Miss Sumpter."

Annoyed with him as much as my fantasies, I smacked his hand away. "I'm not normally a hurdler," I answered, throwing him a sarcastic grin that was more of a grimace.

He inclined his head as he started putting my sock back on. I pulled my foot away and winced again as the movement jolted my ankle.

"It could do with some ice, but should be better tomorrow," he said, wrapping his hand about halfway between my ankle and knee and pulling it back to him.

The action was gentle enough, but the way he would clearly brook no arguments was unfortunately incredibly sexy in how domineering it was. Curse my hormones and kinks. Fucking dishonour on their goddamn cow and everything. I could not be this hot for the guy who was supposed to be proposing, in a mockery of choice for either of them, to my best friend at the end of the summer.

I watched in silence as he almost tenderly replaced my shoe and did it back up.

"Are you still refusing to let me carry you?" he asked.

I could only nod because I needed a minute to get my breath back after having his hands all over my leg. My freaking leg. Jesus Christ. This was ridiculous. It wasn't like I'd never seen a hot guy before. In real life and everything. What was it about *this* arsehole who made me forget my own damned name by just…existing? It was disgusting and I was horrified with myself.

His tongue ran over his lip so damn slowly it could only have been intentional. He knew what he did to me. Whelp, subtle had never been a word used to describe me.

"Force it is," he said, more to himself than me I was sure.

He stood up in one smooth motion, then he was picking me up around the waist like I weighed nothing more than a big ol' bag o' potatoes and slung me over his shoulder.

"What? Do you bench a hundred one handed for just these kinds of situations?" I snarked as he manoeuvred through the branches. It was difficult to deny how obviously careful he was being of my person.

"How many idiots do you think I save?" was his gruff retort.

I shrugged, leaning my elbows on his back. "I dunno. Wouldn't be surprised if I'm the first. I guess you're not as stupid as you look."

"I'm going to regret this," he muttered in Italian before switching back to English. "How do you figure?"

"Because you know Ollie will never marry you if you let me die. Does it chafe something shocking to be saving someone instead of ending them?" I teased.

"*Si*," was all he said,

So, I commented dryly, "Looks like someone carved a path through here," knowing full-well that it had been him and it had left marks. "Some kind of deranged beast, maybe. How many deranged beasts you Vitalis got on this island?"

"The last fucking time I help her," he muttered in Italian.

I smirked. "Fine by me," I answered easily in English. "I mean, I was happy to wait until I could walk. No one asked you to manhandle me, *Maverick*."

"Mav," he spat, like he had no control over it. "Just fucking... Do not call me Maverick. Or Mikhail. And since when do you speak Italian?"

I was going to put the whole name thing on the back burner for it to stew, and answered, "Uh, since my best friend is being stuck with a psychopathic Italian mobster."

"Gangster," he said as he dropped me gently by his car.

I looked at him, his hands still on me helping me to stand. "What?"

He shook his head and muttered something I didn't rightly hear, but I was sure I caught the word for 'joke'.

"Thanks," I begrudgingly admitted.

It was Summer, but there was a breeze and I wasn't dressed for a breeze on the side of a hill.

He inclined his head as he opened the door for me to get in.

"Don't tell me they teach mobsters to be gentlemen. All the easier to woo unsuspecting rivals' women, I suppose."

"Get in the fucking car," he huffed.

I gave him the most sarcastic grimace I could rustle up as I awkwardly angled myself into the car. Unsurprisingly, I was unsteady at best, but Mav's hand was there to help me and I couldn't bring myself to even be overly snarky about it.

I was sore. I was tired. I was getting so damn hungry.

I just wanted to be back at the manor, and bemoaning my excellent fortune to Olive.

My hand still in his, I looked back at him when I was safely sitting on the seat. He inclined his again once, then we seemed to simultaneously agree it was time to disconnect. He closed my door and went around to the driver's side.

We said nothing more as we headed back to the manor.

CHAPTER FOUR

I would have pegged Mav as the 'blast music at the top of the volume button' kind of guy, but the car was eerily silent as we wound our way down that side of that hill.

I didn't mind so much. It let me get lost in the evening, descending on the village ahead of us as the twinkling lights started shining and blinking up at us.

But of course, all good things must come to a hurtling stop. At least, that was my visceral experience of anything remotely good in life. And the golden, definitely not awkward, silence ended as soon as my hungry tummy complained VERY loudly about how long it had been since I'd fed it, and there was no way Mav hadn't heard it.

For a moment, I thought he wasn't going to say anything. And he didn't. But instead of continuing on through the village, he abruptly found a park along the road, turned off the engine and got out. I sat there for a second, assuming this was some kind of mafia drop off situation, and he was just going to be a second. So, I sat, twiddling my thumbs and watching the world go by while I tried very hard to make sure I wasn't looking in any direction Mav might be in. Plausible deniability and all that.

Then, the car door opened, and he was staring at me in frustrated annoyance.

"Are you getting out?" he asked.

I blinked. "Why would I be getting out?"

"Dinner," he said, like it was so obvious. Like we'd spent the whole day discussing it and he'd reminded me at every opportunity so there was no way I forgot.

"Dinner?"

He nodded and stood up, holding the door open for me. "Dinner."

"Aren't we having dinner with your dad and Olive?"

Please say we were having dinner with his dad and Olive. Like, they were meeting us there and I'd just not got the memo because…why wouldn't I have got the memo? Oh yeah, stupid idiot left their phone back at the palazzo on her bed.

"No."

"I'm not dressed for dinner. You said I wasn't even dressed for a *hike*."

He shrugged, like he was saying he could get me into the damned Oscars in my pjs if I wanted. "Get out of the car, Miss Sumpter."

"Get in the car, get out of the car," I muttered. "Make up your damned mind."

My stomach chose that moment to protest again, as though it knew Mav was promising the cure to what ailed it, and was daring me to keep pushing back. Well, who was I to deny it?

"You're paying," I warned him, as I started to swing my legs out.

As he held out a helpful arm, he inclined his head. "Of course."

I blinked, somewhat surprised by his simple agreement. "How thoughtful of you," I said sarcastically.

He turned a cocky smirk on me. "Of course…you didn't bring your wallet."

I really should have known it wasn't simple agreement. That was on me.

"Oh, sorry," I gasped. "Did the bunnies have their market stall day today? How ever could I have missed Signora Coniglia's strawberry jam!"

His eyes narrowed, but something dangerously seductive and alluring burned bright and deep in them. "Are you always this charming?"

"I am," I sassed as I flicked my plait over my shoulder. "Thank you for noticing."

Something akin to a smile ghosted his lips as he helped take my weight and led me to a tiny little cafe that was little more than a hole in the wall.

"Are *you* always this charming?" I turned on him.

He shook his head. "Never."

I tried to hold back a laugh, but a snigger escaped me and I had to bite my lip to stop it exploding even further. The sheer audacity that he was trying to claim he was charming, or even more amusing that he was trying to make a joke of it, was an intimacy I shouldn't encourage but desperately wanted to.

Mav and the owner of the cafe chatted in rapid Italian I didn't strain myself to follow, then we were directed to a table – one of about five – and presented with menus.

"So, what's good eats here?" I asked him, pretending the situation was at all normal.

"Would it surprise you if I said pasta?"

"You know, it wouldn't."

He inclined his head and held two fingers up to the owner.

Normally, I'd be heavily annoyed by someone – especially a man I couldn't say I really liked – ordering for me. On the other hand, it wasn't like Mav was the first and I doubted he'd be the last. Plus, he was the local and I was the tourist. In this situation, I was actually quite happy to let the local order me what he thought was worth trying.

While I feigned my calm exterior, my mind was racing, my heart was thundering, my hands were feeling kinda sweaty, and I got serious restless leg syndrome. All while a smile of the totally nervous, ridiculously excited, goofy happy kind tried to break open my whole face. Like this was a date or something equally stupid and naïve.

Two plates of pasta, two glasses and a bottle of wine was placed between us. Mav nodded in thanks but didn't take his eyes from me.

He was studying me intently and, for once, I couldn't tell what was going through his head. Mostly because he wasn't looking at me like I was an idiot or irritatingly disobedient. He wasn't obviously thinking dirty thoughts as his eyes roved my body, eliciting wild ones in me. He didn't look angry or bored or like he was two seconds away from killing someone. His grey-green eyes were soft as he shuffled his food absently and popped some in his mouth as those very same eyes never left my face.

"What?" I asked, feeling the uncertain nerves tugging harder at my lips. I made do with tucking a non-existent piece of hair behind my ear and focussing on my dinner.

He shrugged. "You are not what I expected."

I let myself smile then as I sat back in my seat. "If that isn't the oldest line in the book, Mav," I chuckled.

He ran his tongue over his lip and nodded. "It wasn't meant to be a line."

"What was it meant to be, then?" I asked as I leant my elbows on the suddenly very small table between us.

"Miss Carlione. Exactly as I expected," he said as he poured the wine "You are nothing like I expected."

"What were you expecting? Plain Jane tomboy with zero social skills and a Victorian fashion sense?"

Humour sparked in his eyes. "As beautiful and desirable as you are, I am sure you would be just as sexy in your…Victorian fashion."

I swallowed and chewed my lip. "Is that so?"

He inclined his head. "It took me…off guard. And I am not easily surprised."

"So, I'm *too* sexy for you?" I said incredulously, while madly stomping down an eruption of flutters and skitters and tingles that raced each other through my whole body.

His eye brow quirked suggestively as a very tiny smile lit his lips. "I promise I can handle you."

Awkwardly, I checked the time on my watch, just to give me a purpose in looking away other than I was about to combust under his scrutiny. As I saw my battery level, I was super mature and let out a snigger.

"What?' he asked and I was sure I imagined the smile in his voice.

I shook my head as I lifted my wrist towards him. "No. Just… My battery's on sixty-nine percent…" I trailed off, feeling like an idiot, but still fighting a smile.

He blinked like he wasn't sure if I was serious, then one corner of his lip tipped up as he blew out a soft laugh. Then the other corner tipped, not quite as high, and he actually chuckled roughly. I think my heart actually stopped inside my person.

Mav was a stunning specimen of humanity. It didn't hurt that he was dark and dangerous, and totally unobtainable. All of which was *exactly* my type. But that smile? That unguarded, actual smile?

I had never tingled like that before.

I cleared my throat. As I was trying to work out what to say next, he refilled my empty glass. I noticed he'd barely touched his.

"Trying to get me drunk?" I teased. "Lower my inhibitions?"

He smirked. "We both know it doesn't matter if we're drunk or sober."

I admired his gumption. Because there was no way I didn't know what he was referring to. But it hit a little too close to home to joke about. He was a dick in every situation but, inexplicably, this one, and he was supposed to marry my best friend. Even if there was no risk either of them would ever catch feelings, there was no world where me hooking up with him wouldn't be weird and awkward later. So, I just couldn't think about him like that.

"I thought it…gentlemanly to pace myself since I'm driving you home," he answered the real question.

I nodded as I took a very large sip of mine. "No. Of course. Makes sense."

Mav leant towards me, and I felt his hand on my knee under the table. "If your inhibitions happen to lower far enough that…"

He left the end of that sentence hanging wildly. Coupled with that sexy half-smirk and heated twinkle in his eyes. I was in trouble. I forced a deep breath to keep my breathing, for the most part, steady.

I blew out and plastered on a wide, nonchalant smile. "So, Mav.

Tell me exactly what it is you gangsters do all day."

Rather than be disappointed I hadn't risen to the direct challenge, he seemed pleased that I'd issued a different one. He pulled away again and went back to his food with a satisfied tilt to his lips.

"What makes you think I would talk business with you?" he asked, dragging his teeth over his fork very suggestively.

"The fact that our very acquaintance is business."

"That's not all it is."

Oh, he was pushing the boundaries, and I liked it. If he were any other generic douche bag, I'd have jumped him in a heartbeat, we'd use each other to get what we wanted, then we could both go our separate ways. But he wasn't any other generic douche bag. And, all going well – using the term loosely – we weren't going to be able to go our separate ways.

"That's all it is," I said, aiming for firm but apologetic and disappointed snuck in against my will.

"It doesn't have to be."

I pinned his eyes with mine. "Business, Mav…" I reminded him what we were supposed to be talking about.

He inclined his head. "*Bene*. Business. Do you want me to start with how many men I killed last week?"

I bit my lip against a full smile. "You can start wherever you like," I told him, showing him that I wasn't going to be scared off my questions.

What better way to protect Olive than to get the information straight from the horse's mouth? Or, in this case, the mouth of the horse's son. Daniel had told me a lot. I wanted to see what he'd kept from me.

And Mav didn't disappoint.

Some of the information disappointed. Like the fact that they had some legitimate businesses as well as the shady ones. I mean, boring.

But, as we ate and drank, we talked. About his father's business, or as much as he was willing to tell me. About Olive. About me. About Olive and me at school. Things we liked. Things we didn't. Had I been a better wing woman, I would have focussed on the things Olive in particular liked, but I kept coming back to things we both liked or did together.

"*Dolci*?" he asked when the prima and secondi were both done and two bottles of wine were empty, mainly curtesy of me.

I didn't need to know Italian to figure out what that meant. I shook my head. "As delicious as I'm sure it would be, I seriously overdid the main."

He grinned. "Amateur."

I tried not to smile in response. "Tourist," I corrected him.

He shrugged. "No matter. You know for next time, *si*."

I wasn't going to ask him to expand on the whole idea of a 'next time'. So, I just said, "*Si*."

He nodded. "*Mettili sul mio conto*," he said to the owner, who just inclined his head. The he stood up and held his hand out to me. "Come."

Mav helped me back to the car and already my ankle was feeling better. I hoped it wasn't just a placebo effect caused by the wine.

"Back to the *palazzo*, or can I interest you in something more…scenic?" he purred when we got to the car.

I turned to him. Scenic sounded good. I wanted to say scenic. Instead, I said, "*Palazzo*."

His body leaned into mine again, pressing me into the body of his car. "Are you sure?"

"You think you can just take whatever you want, don't you?" I said. Yes, it was a little bit of a challenge, but I did attempt to deliver it like a reprimand.

"I *can* just take whatever I want…" he said slowly as his nose ran over my cheek.

Oh, and I believed it. Not only that, but I firmly believed most people in his life would kill themselves giving him whatever he wanted. I was very close to giving him whatever he wanted. Not in the least because I was quite convinced that it would get me what I wanted, too. Goddamn. Yeah, I liked it. Aware every feminist just died inside, I still had to admit I liked it.

"But you like that. Don't you?" His hushed whisper across my lips made my nipples tighten while I wondered if he could read my mind. "You want me to take what I want, Echo. Don't you?"

I literally had no words. I wanted him to take what he wanted. I shouldn't and I couldn't because his future was Olive. Even if she was less attracted to him than she was to a wet towel, she was his future and I couldn't get in the way of that. Anything more than this unacted upon hate-fuelled lust between us would just make everything so…messy.

And yet, more was honestly the only thing I wanted every time I looked at him. Every time I thought about him. Every time we found ourselves in potentially compromising situations.

Selfishly, I couldn't lie to him. Even to tease him or sass him or play at flirting disguised as insults. I could still feel his hand on my leg as he checked my wounds. I couldn't stop thinking about the way he'd smiled, the cocky mischief in his eyes, over dinner. Everything in my mind and senses was Mikhail Vitali and even my sense of self-preservation wasn't strong enough to push him away.

His hand slid up my body to grip my throat. I lifted my chin to look him in the eyes.

"It would be so easy…" he groaned. "So easy to take what I want."

"You want me, Mikhail?" I whispered, my lips brushing his.

His hand tightened. "Let's not pretend the feeling isn't mutual."

Lust at first sight. Seemed I was right, and I hadn't been the only one who'd felt it. If only that felt like good news.

"Do it, then," I challenged, fully expecting him to get angry with me and push away.

He didn't.

Oh, Mav pushed, but he pushed me into the car even further. His knee pressed between my legs, and mine inadvertently hugged it. We stared into each other's eyes for the space of a very tense heartbeat.

Then his hand slid up to my chin and he crushed his lips to mine.

Holy shit.

I just melted.

Butterflies might have taken flight from my stomach, but there was a flock of something much larger that erupted in my heart and sent tingles skittering down my arms. One hand braced on his arm before it slid up to his shoulder, and the other fisted his shirt near his hip. He leant into me as the hand on my chin trailed around my neck to cradle my head. As his body pressed into mine, I felt him hard against my hip.

He could simply lift me up. Or we could fall into his back seat.

No. There wasn't much of a back seat. His front seat would probably do. I could just climb on top and…

What in the hell was wrong with me?

I pushed against him and slapped him across the face.

We were both breathing heavily, and my head and heart were racing. But Mav was grinning, like he'd got exactly what he wanted from me. He licked his bottom lip agonisingly slowly as he looked me up and down.

"Game on, little nymph."

He bit his lip like he was trying not to smile, then huffed a rough laugh and went around to the driver's door.

My cheeks flamed in annoyed embarrassment that I'd so easily given in. Of course, that wasn't the only thing burning in me. Even deeper, was desire. And all it wanted was to unleash Mav on my body like he was the only thing for the rest of my life who could sate me.

Well, I wasn't giving into it or him.

I ignored him the whole way back to the palazzo. Olive met us and followed my unusually cranky person up to my room and I begrudgingly told her about the wall incident, but left out the majority of what followed. But the wall incident alone was enough to satisfy her curiosity, and she fully believed that was enough to put me in such a mood.

It felt like shit not to tell her everything, but I knew her. She'd either tell me to go for it and then I'd be uncomfortable about her future with Mav, or she'd be uncomfortable about what it meant for her future with Mav. And I didn't want to face either of those conversations.

CHAPTER FIVE

I woke up the next morning, burning hot. The remnants of my dream still echoed in me and my whole body still tingled from Dream-Mav's epic touch. I didn't remember the specifics about much, except the epic movie trailer playlist was the only one appropriate as the soundtrack.

I bent my knees up and lent my head on the tent the sheets made, breathing heavily.

If there was a morning that Olive wasn't in my room before I was awake, I was glad it had been that one. Lusting after Mav was complicated. Actually acting on it would become hell. There was no point and yet, all I wanted was to continue our kiss from the night before.

I groaned in frustration. "I am the worst!"

I got dressed and wrenched my door open with a little more gusto than necessary.

Olive smiled at me quizzically as she was coming out of her door across the hall. "Should I call for a doctor?"

I frowned. "What? Why?"

She laughed. "Because you are voluntarily out of bed, and it's not even nine."

I huffed. "Couldn't sleep."

"Your ankle bothering you?" she asked as we made our way to the breakfast room.

I shook my head. "I can still feel a bit of pain in it, but it's a lot better than it was."

She nudged me playfully. "Good thing Maverick came along when he did."

"Mav," I said without thinking.

"What?"

I shrugged. "Nothing. Yes. *Just* my luck that Mr Grumpy Sarcastic Pants happened to be passing as I took a nosedive off a wall."

Olive's pure, bright laugh tinkled over the marble of the entry hall. "Pot meet kettle."

I gave her a smile. I knew what I was. "Fine. But I still think I would have preferred to walk back."

She linked her arm with mine as we made our way to our seats. We were, for possibly the first time in my life, the first people in the breakfast room other than staff. Olive barely paid them any mind, but I nodded in greeting, and they returned it as they went about sorting coffee. They were being very tolerant about the foreigners' coffee preferences, and I appreciated it.

Rico was the next one in with a, "Good morning, ladies. How did you sleep?"

Olive engaged in pleasant small talk while I inhaled caffeine. I'd managed to avoid a full-blown hangover after dinner the night before, but I still felt a bit fuzzy around the edges.

"Where is Adriana?" I heard Olive ask Rico.

"She is packing. She decided to head home after we're done

today. Her husband's work needed him back and she felt they'd been apart long enough."

"Aw, that's sweet. Have they been married long?"

"About six years."

I tuned back out as Mav walked in the door with his brother. Vin – which he'd insisted we call him – was like a pale attempt at a copy of Mav. Like if I'd tried drawing Mav from memory with the artistic skills I only half-heartedly nurtured while Olive was busy mastering hers. Mav was the sort of portrait Olive would come up with. Vin was probably better than what I could hope to accomplish actually, to be fair to him.

Like their father, Vin had dark brown eyes, and the dark brown hair that seemed prevalent in their family. He was good-looking with a strong nose and jawline. He was tall and slim. That morning he favoured cream trousers – bold – and a button-down polo with thick stripes of green and tan, tucked in. As a package, I could see it held appeal. It just didn't appeal specifically to me. He was attractive without me being attracted to him.

Which is more than could be said for his brother.

Because, even with that knowing, shit-stirring smirk at the corner of his lips and the condescending humour shining in his eyes, I was attracted to Mav. That morning, he was back in dark trousers and a dark button shirt. Funny how he never wore jeans around his father.

A waiter bringing me breakfast forced me to look away from Mav and I took the opportunity to studiously ignore him and the rest of the table. Which only lasted until Rico said my name.

"Echo, we missed you at dinner last night," Rico said slowly.

I looked up at him, my fork paused and my mouth wide open.

He was smiling at me and I knew it was supposed to be friendly. But it wasn't friendly. It was expectant. It was humoured. It was like he knew he was putting me on the spot and he loved it.

I lowered my fork as I closed my mouth and sat up straighter. "Yeah. Sorry, I wasn't here."

Rico picked up his wine glass and sat back in his chair with a shrug. "No matter. There will be more dinners. What is more important is that you are okay."

I blinked. "Okay?"

He nodded. "After your…fall."

Without any food or drink in my person, the only thing left for me to choke on in surprise was my own spit. Olive huffed humouredly beside me. I tried hard not to cough and felt my eyes watering.

"Fall," I wheezed with a nod.

"Yes. I heard there was an unfortunate incident between you and a wall." He looked at his eldest son, as though confirming what he'd been told.

My eyes slid to Mav, and I frowned. There was an arrogant tilt to one corner of his mouth as he shovelled food into his face. *Snitch!* Ugh, and why was he so insufferably attractive while he was clearly getting off on my clumsiness and pain?

I took a breath. "Uh. Yes. There was."

Rico steepled his fingers in front of his chest. "Was it your *first* incident with a wall?"

I scratched my head absently. "I mean, define incident. It's not like I've never…met a wall before…"

What?

Olive smiled prettily at everyone. "Coco's been dying to go for a ramble since we knew we were coming. And the first time she got to, Maverick had to save her from falling off a wall!"

God damn her. Why was she so good at sounding like she was talking about the weather while having a laugh at me at the same time?

Rico grinned and I had to admit that, objectively, the man was attractive. "Echo, you enjoy the outdoors?"

I took a sip of water and managed a breath without resorting to spluttering coughing. "Nature has never let me down, Rico." I inclined my head. "That and Olive."

"You are lucky to have such a strong bond with such a strong friend," Rico said, and seemed to genuinely be sincere.

Olive nudged my knee with hers under the table and smiled. "I honestly forget we're not sisters sometimes."

"Yin and yang," Rico said happily.

Olive's smile grew. "Yin and yang."

He nodded. "Good. Now. Plans for the day, Echo, while Olive is busy?"

Olive nodded. "She's staying closer to home today."

I grumbled at my breakfast, "She *can* speak for herself."

"And very well," Rico agreed. "I can have a man drive you to the village if you'd like? I'm sure the two of you haven't been able to empty all the stock yet."

"I think I'm all shopped out for now," I told him. "I was thinking I might explore the grounds. I've been looking for an excuse to have a look at the vineyard and winery."

"Why?" Mav asked. "There are no cliffs out there."

Because, in one of my many other lives, I quite liked the idea of being a vintner actually. Not that he needed to know that.

I shot him a sarcastic grimace. "Maybe it's market day."

"Then best you do not forget your wallet."

I huffed and ignored Olive's questioning smile. "Best not."

"Now that is settled," Rico said, amusement dancing in his voice. "Olive, dear, shall we be on our way?"

I hadn't asked exactly what Rico had planned for Olive that day, but I understood it was some bonding thing with him and Adriana that he didn't want to impose upon me. I was all for that. I had nothing against Adriana – I barely knew her from a bar of soap – but I was sure she hadn't warmed to me at all.

Olive and Rico got up, followed by Vin who was off to do who knew what, made their goodbyes, and left me and Mav sitting at the table, all alone in the breakfast room.

Very slowly, he leant one elbow, then the other, on the table and leant towards me. "How easy to clear this table and throw you down on it."

"If a kiss got you slapped, what do you expect that will get you?" came out much shakier than I'd intended.

But, I mean, could anyone blame me? The idea of him just sweeping the whole table clear in a fit of sexual passion over little old me? Then having me among the remnants of the breakfast things? There was cream on the table. Thick, whipped, fresh cream.

Bad, Echo.

That cocky smirk ghosted at one corner of his lips. "Why don't you show me?"

I rolled my eyes as I picked up my coffee. "I bet you'd like that, wouldn't you?"

He nodded. "*Mi piacerebbe*."

"Well, one can't fault your honesty, I suppose."

He popped a strawberry into his mouth like he knew I'd been thinking about doing nasty things with the cream only moments ago. "You will find little fault with me, Miss Sumpter. I can promise you that."

"Really? How about your personality? Or your manners? Your annoying cockiness?"

There went that perfect, full half-smile. "My...*cockiness* will more than make up for it," he promised, as though he was ninety percent certain he was using the right word, but couldn't entirely be sure because his grasp of the English language was tenuous at best. Sure it was.

I bit my lip. Hard. Or I was at risk of laughing. When I had a modicum of self-control left, I said, quite deadpan, "And now you've built up all this expectation. I couldn't possibly test your theory for fear of disappointment."

He flashed me a grin. "*Bene.* If you don't need me, I have some business to attend."

I shrugged, confused and aroused at his sudden change of subject. "Sure."

"Do not go falling off any walls while I am gone."

Another lip-bite in lieu of smiling. "I can't make any promises."

He shook his head, a soft hint of a smile at his lips and I swore I heard him mutter, "*la mia morte*." Then he nodded. "I will see you later, Miss Sumpter."

I gave him my sweetest smile. "I wish I could say I looked

forward to it."

He licked his lip, but the corner still tilted. "*Naturalmente*. Good morning, Miss Sumpter."

I politely inclined my head. "Good morning, *Signore* Vitali."

He nodded once in return, then stuck his hands in his pockets and strode out purposefully. Those hands in those pockets made the material of his trousers pull tight around his arse and I did not hate the view as he left.

"And then there was one." I sighed a heavy breath as I sipped at my coffee and wondered exactly what I was going to do with my day.

Explore the grounds seemed like a perfectly plausible option and, were I to be very me and get lost again, at least everyone else would have a vague idea of where I was.

The estate was, annoyingly, gorgeous. I couldn't deny that. The whole 'holiday' was turning into annoying gorgeousness everywhere I looked. The guys. The architecture. The shopping. The bloody scenery.

Forget the rambling hills and valleys, I could spend the rest of the summer just getting happily lost on the grounds of the Vitali palazzo. Find me under a tree or down a pathway or dancing among the grape vines.

The whole place gave one ideas about claiming their destiny and actually having a life not lived for someone else. But I loved Olive. Spending my life by her side was a choice I'd made. No one would begrudge me going off to university without her and chasing that degree in Language and Linguistics, meet a nice guy, travel the world, maybe meet a few more less nice guys, a few more nice guys, and finally settle down some day.

That wasn't who I was.

As much as I told myself that we were only with the Vitalis for the Summer, I knew we were here for life. I knew the plan was for us to study our university degrees online; Olive in Animal Behaviour and me in Language. I don't think Olive knew much about what she planned to do with a degree in Animal Behaviour, but it was that or Visual Art and the science part of her brain had won out.

I paused in my rambling and looked around. The vineyards were in a vague 'ahead' direction, even if I couldn't see them just at that moment because of the way the path meandered.

There was something very nice about just getting lost in my thoughts as I wandered. Even with all the shit in my past, I enjoyed just being in my own head. I'd been lucky that, unlike my mum, all my demons manifested externally and physically – such as poor life choices and heavy sarcasm – less so internally and mentally.

I'd found my way onto a gravel path that wound under trellised vines and narrow paths like they'd been forgotten and left to grow rampant long ago. Or maybe forbidden. Naturally, that idea appealed to me greatly, so I continued even when I'd have to climb through a tiny hole among the vine branches.

I didn't even care what was on the other side. Maybe it was a cliff and Mav would get the last laugh when this idiot finally fell to her death.

Once most of my body was on the other side, of course my foot got stuck.

"Oh, come on!" I muttered as I pulled on my leg, making me hop on the other. "Why me? Why does this always happen…?"

I finally pried my foot loose and spun wildly with the momentum.

As my foot hit the ground again, I overbalanced slightly in an effort to remain standing. Which I did. Just. Still counts. Very proud. As I stood up straight, I double fist pumped the air in celebration of my minor victory. I also finally realised I hadn't been alone since I first started worming my way through the vines. Less proud.

"…to me," I eventually finished my sentence, as I dropped my arms and looked at the five people all watching me intently in the small, walled courtyard I was now in.

I swallowed hard and nodded.

Mav and Antonio were accompanied by a third suited muscle I knew by sight alone. They were standing around two other suited muscles, both of whom were on their knees with what looked like their wrists bound behind them. Mav had a gun to the head of one of them. And his eyes were locked onto mine like he dared me to have a comment on the 'business' he'd had to attend.

Antonio's eyes darted to Mav, like he wasn't sure how to go about damage control, or if he even should.

I looked back to Mav, whose eyes never left mine.

Then a loud crack reverberated around us, and I flinched, but didn't look away from him.

Brains splattered as the guy at Mav's feet toppled sideways. The other guy looked like he was about to cry.

Mav said something to Antonio and their accomplice, too low for me to hear at that distance, before he holstered his gun and came over to me, like 'wasn't it a pleasant day, and have you seen the roses this year?'.

"It is perhaps inadvisable for you to wander the grounds unaccompanied, Miss Sumpter," Mav said in that sinful yet derisive tone as he stopped in front of me.

I bristled but hid it behind mock-innocence. "Oh, you think a little murder is going to worry me? Bless your little cotton socks."

Surprise lit his eyes, but he kept his face haughty and superior. "My father can arrange someone to…look after you."

"To kill me or babysit me?"

"Babysit you." Although, the idea of me thinking they'd kill me seemed to amuse him.

I frowned. "Like I need a babysitter. Why? Is your whole island secret murder hollows and cliffs for idiots to fall off?" I retorted hotly.

My annoyance was obviously getting him off, and I couldn't rightly bring myself to cool down.

"Something like that. Miss Carlione would hate for something to happen to you."

"I mean, I might also mind, but let's not worry about a little nobody like me."

The corner of his lip tipped ever so slightly. "No, let's not."

Very maturely, I smacked him in the chest. "Ugh, you're insufferable."

His hand wrapped around my wrist gently. "Thank you." And pulled me to him. "There are sides to our business, to us…we do not want you to see."

I got the feeling 'we' wasn't the word he'd been going to say. It felt like he'd started to say 'I'.

I leant into him, making our noses almost brush. "You might believe Olive is delicate and naïve, but I doubt I've ever given you reason to think the same about me. If you think I haven't spent years learning everything Daniel would tell me about your family, then you were woefully underprepared for me. I'm here–"

He stepped into me, making me stumble backwards. He had to put his arm around me to keep me standing, which only served to pin me to his body. My heart started beating erratically as I looked up at him in question.

"Oh, I was definitely unprepared for you," he whispered as he searched my eyes. His lips dropped to graze the briefest of kisses across mine as he continued, "And I've been playing catch up ever since."

His words seemed to descend over me, wrapping around my body, permeating my very skin until the tendrils of his enticement closed around my very heart and seemed to jump start it back into proper sinus rhythm. Mav Vitali had a power over me no one had ever held before, and he'd taken it without me even realising. But I saw it, deep in his eyes; he'd unconsciously given me the same power over him.

I pushed against his chest, feeling ruffled in more ways than one. My eyes darted to where Antonio still stood over the dead body. The third muscle had left with the other guy. Antonio wouldn't meet my eyes. He was very decidedly acting like he wasn't paying any attention whatsoever to his boss with a woman not his intended. I was sure it wasn't the first time since we'd arrived, but it would be the last time that woman was me.

This thing between Mav and I could very easily be more than just lust. It was one kiss away from being pure obsession. Which, standing this close to him, sounded perfect. Ideal. Where do I sign?

But God. The complications Future Me would have to face.

I wasn't against some whirlwind Summer Romance that shattered my heart into a thousand jagged pieces when it ended, but knowing he'd have to move on with Olive? Even if I was sure she'd wholeheartedly support Present Me's life choices without thinking of what the future held?

Both Olive and I deserved better.

I shook my head at Mav, then pushed passed him and got out of that courtyard as fast as I could.

CHAPTER SIX

"Come on!" I heard Olive's perky voice. "Get up."

Sun blasted behind my closed eyes as she, no doubt, flung my curtains open like she was in a Disney movie. I scrunched my eyes further closed and buried my face in my blankets.

"What God forsaken time do you call this?" I mumbled.

"Nine," Olive answered as she ripped the blankets off me. "A perfectly God respectable time of day to be getting up. Especially for those of us going on a picnic."

I looked at her blearily. "Sorry, we're what?"

She went to my wardrobe and pulled it open. "Rico has organised a lovely picnic for us, Maverick, and Antonio."

"So, he's ordered Maverick to put in some effort, then?" I teased.

She smirked as she rifled through my clothes. "Something like that."

"Well, who am I to pass up a picnic?"

She smiled back at me. "You mean, who are you to pass up flirting with Antonio?"

I never claimed to be a good person, but I was going to do my damnedest to make sure Olive didn't guess I was more keen to watch her intended be a total arsehole than flirt with a semi-respectable, far more suitable, and much more reciprocal candidate like Antonio.

So, I grinned. "Can't let you have all the fun this summer."

Olive pulled a dress out of my wardrobe and I lost all sense of joviality.

"No."

She gave me the 'I'm not negotiating' face.

I shook my head. "No."

She doubled down on the face.

I sighed as I flailed my hands in defeat. "Fine, but if you suggest heels to go with it, I'm throwing myself off the nearest cliff."

She rolled her eyes. "Heels for a picnic. Are you mad?"

"Only in the most endearing sense."

"Wedges, please."

I groaned and pulled the blankets back over my head. "You do remember I fell off a wall not two days ago?"

"Fine. Sandals, but it's my last offer."

I groaned more loudly.

"You were fine gallivanting all over the vineyards yesterday," she reminded me, and I frowned to myself.

Damn Past Me making trouble for Present Me.

I threw the blankets off again. "Gallivanting?" I sassed and she grinned at me.

"Yes, gallivanting."

I looked her over and decided that, if I had to wear a dress, at least I wouldn't look out of place because she was wearing something very similar to what she'd picked out for me.

"I suppose," I said pointedly, "you expect me to sit sideways all demurely and make sure I don't accidentally flash anyone my knickers?"

She nodded. "I do."

I sighed, "Fine!" loudly and obnoxiously. "The things I do for you."

She patted my knee. "And I appreciate it. How are we doing your hair?"

"Oh, are we pretending I have a say in the matter?"

Her smile was infectious. "No. But I can play Mrs Hellfire and tell you that you're hardly going to have an suitors lining up with your denim and wild ways."

I snorted at her impression of the governess who'd taken over after my mother's episode. I'd started calling her Mrs Hellfire – behind her back obviously, even I wasn't brave enough to say it to her face – after a single day. Olive had joined me about a week later. Or rather, Olive had stopped telling me to knock it off after a week.

"Well then, Mrs Hellfire. I shall remind you that any man turned off by my denim and wild ways will instantly turn me off and I'd be glad to avoid his attentions. Thank you."

"Lucky then that Maverick seems to like you in anything."

I tried inhaling and swallowing at the same time and ended up spluttering. Not just dignified, but very inconspicuous as well, for sure.

"I couldn't care less what Mav thinks of me."

"I think it's very telling that he saves you and suddenly you're all 'Mav' this and 'Mav' that."

I snorted as I gathered my thoughts. "It tells you that mere minutes with the man made me lose my goddamned mind."

"I don't know why you're so adamant you're not attracted to him."

"I don't know why you're so adamant I am."

She gave me a look that clearly told me she knew far more than I wanted her to, but she was going to keep her mouth shut until I told her the truth because that would teach me a valuable lesson about honesty. In turn, I flipped her off.

"I suppose you'll tell me that you're shagging the kitchen staff?" she said as she unnecessarily helped haul me out of bed.

"Yeah, no. When have I had time to organise a hook up? We've had dinners and debriefing and hanging out to do."

"And yet you've found time to get lost in the wilderness and fall off a wall, and go on a full-day tour of the winery without getting drunk?"

I shrugged. "What can I say? Sex is the same anywhere. Walls and wineries, not so much."

"You need to sort out your priorities," she said gravely.

"I only *nearly* got expelled," I reminded her.

"Yes, because Daddy paid a lot of money to keep you enrolled."

I smiled fondly. "I wonder how the new aquatics building is working out?"

"Get dressed. You'll need coffee before we leave."

I gasped sarcastically as I wandered to the bathroom. "It's like you've met me before!"

She laughed warmly. "It's like you've annoyed me before, you mean," she called after me.

I was dressed and yielding to the ministrations of Olive's hair curling when there was a knock on the door.

"Come in," Olive called, and I glared at her.

"We don't want any more well-wishers–" I started, but she

threatened me with the curling iron and I shut up.

Saracco walked in with a tray of what looked and smelled like coffee. "*Signore* Vitali thought *Signorina* Sumpter may need room service," he explained, and I tried not to wonder which Signore Vitali had thought that.

I smiled at him in the mirror. "*Grazie*, Saracco. You didn't have to bring it for us."

He inclined his head as he put the tray on a table. "My pleasure, *Signorina* Sumpter. There is tea for *Signorina* Carlione."

"*Grazie*," Olive said with a bright smile. "Coco has been quite trying already this morning."

I rolled my eyes to Saracco conspiratorially. "Duh. The very presence of 'morning' should have clued you in."

She laughed, Saracco smiled then ducked out of the room.

Thankfully, I was allowed to drink my coffee while she finished gussying me up, as long as I didn't tilt my head. Then there was a change of clothes required and, as a result, I was banned from finishing my coffee until she was done. It was cold by then, but I was pretty sure I was going to need the caffeine if I was expected to not murder my best friend's future husband.

And I was right, because the man seemed made solely to annoy, infuriate, tease, and tempt me. He found me by the stream later that afternoon after I'd wandered off on a wild strawberry hunt. The main food and drink had been consumed, and we were all in the digesting stage before really diving into the sweet stuff.

"Didn't Daddy ever warn you of the dangers of wandering off by yourself?" he asked.

Damn. That. Voice.

I spun to face him. "Didn't Daddy ever warn you about sneaking up on your enemy?"

His eyebrow rose. "We're enemies?"

"Any man with an obsession about me wandering off, is looked upon with suspicion and scrutiny. We women need to be careful."

He inclined his head. "Yes, you do." Somehow, he managed to make it sound like both an insult and an argument.

"I'm quite capable of *not* injuring myself. I was fine yesterday."

He thumbed his nose before crossing his arms over his chest. "You got yourself into trouble."

I scoffed, knowing what he was referring to. "Not as much trouble as the guy you *killed*," I pointed out.

I heard Olive's bright laughter and looked back towards the blanket. I could just make her and Antonio out, dazzling in the sunshine through the trees. I suspected Mav and I were less easily spied on.

"He betrayed my father," was his explanation.

I shrugged as I crossed my own arms. "It's not for me to tell you how to do business. If I had a job, I certainly wouldn't want you coming in and telling me how to do it. Like being strangely obsessed that I don't wander off and hurt myself. That would just be weird and kind of condescending, wouldn't it?"

Humour danced in his eyes at my sarcasm. "This job. What is it?"

"What?"

"Your job. In this imaginary scenario in your head where I *don't* tell you what to do."

I huffed as I looked back over the stream. "Translation."

"Translation?"

I nodded and, feeling like this conversation might be in for the long haul, helped myself to a seat. Mav followed suit. I crossed my legs, habit making me tuck my skirt between them. He kept his bent and leant his arms on his knees.

"I figure with all the jet-setting and travel and 'networking' you and Olive will be expected to do, someone she trusts needs to be able to help her translate with foreign languages. When I'm not needed, I was thinking I might freelance translations of novels. Romance, of course. The dirtier, the better."

He said nothing about that, but I heard the amusement in the words he did say. "And just how many languages do you plan on speaking?"

I shrugged. "I speak four already. Fluently," I added, in case he was thinking of making a quip. "I'll learn two more during my degree, plus minor in Linguistics."

"Why do I never hear you speaking anything other than English if you speak three other languages?"

I felt my cheeks heat and looked down the stream in the other direction to him in the hopes he might not notice. "I'm working on it."

"On what?"

I sighed and snuck a look at him out of the corner of my eye. He totally saw, as he was looking right at me.

"I have…stage fright, I guess, when it comes to speaking other languages. I don't know why. I just…get really self-conscious, and I don't want to be that rude, ignorant foreigner who comes in and butchers a beautiful language."

"And what is Linguistics?" he asked, like he knew I didn't really want to expand on my flaws any more than necessary.

"Unfortunately nothing to do with pasta," I joked, which earned me a small laugh from him. "No. Uh, it's the study of human language. What language is, why, and using that to understand communication, culture, society and humanity." I shrugged like it was nothing. "It's always fascinated me."

"It sounds…interesting."

I laughed, "I think so. But then I just like learning. In another life, I'd be an historian, maybe an archaeologist, and get lost in the mysteries of the past. In another, I'd like to live in the countryside and make amazing wine, then again maybe that would ruin my appreciation for it. In another, I'd raise horses, although I've never ridden one. Maybe I could be a perfumer, if my nose was any good. I could have been a renowned chef, if I had more interest in gastronomy than ingestion. In yet another, I'd be an engineer, although my brain isn't that kind of sciencey really. I was never really any good with Maths, not like Olive. When they introduced letters, I was out and she was just getting started."

Mav looked over his shoulder where we could still hear Olive and Antonio talking and laughing. "She's very intelligent."

I wasn't sure if it was a question or a statement.

"She is. She hides it, though. Thinks that Society will shun her if they find out she's not just a pretty face. I think it was all Bobby Kramer's fault."

"Who is Bobby Kramer?"

I smiled, remembering that time of our lives. "It was stupid, really. We were probably fourteen or fifteen, maybe. Olive didn't really date, as a rule. Daniel told her young she was supposed to marry you, and I guess she spent her life waiting for Prince Charming and didn't really think about other guys like that."

"And then, I turn up," he teased.

I bit my lip as I nodded. "Imagine our disappointment," I sassed. "Anyway, then there was Bobby. I knew Olive liked him. She didn't mean to. It just happened."

"It usually does," he agreed.

I ignored the thinly veiled meaning behind those words. "And he seemed to like her, too. Then, she beat him on a Maths test. Like, he came second and even his mark was only seventy, and she got a ninety-eight. I think that was the first time everyone realised she was actually packing some serious brains. But Bobby's pride was wounded, and he was a dick. No way could Olive be pretty *and* smart. She must have cheated. Or, even more viciously, maybe she'd done something to make the teacher give her such a good grade. Even the idiots like me could tell what he wanted everyone to think she'd done to make the teacher mark her so highly."

"He sounds like an arsehole."

"Pot meet kettle?" I suggested and he cocked his head in question. I waved my hand. "Just means… Something about the pot calling the kettle black, when the pot is also black and possibly even more black. I'm not sure. Either way, basically it's ironic that an arsehole is calling someone else an arsehole."

"So, being an arsehole automatically makes me unable to judge if another is an arsehole? Does this mean you're incapable of judging who hides behind scorn and sarcasm?"

I narrowed my eyes at him. "Touché, sir."

"You do not argue?"

"I do not," I said begrudgingly. "I know who I am."

"That is a very attractive quality."

I knew exactly what he was trying to say. He was making a point of reminding me he was attracted to me, while suggesting that Olive was less attractive because he perceived she lacked a quality I owned. While it was nice to hear I was the pretty one for once, he was wrong about Olive.

"Olive knows who she is," I defended her.

He huffed as a laugh teased at his lips. "Interesting that your mind should go to Olive when I didn't mention her."

I rubbed my arms self-consciously. "I thought you needed the reminder."

"You thought to play wing woman even as you're thinking about me throwing you on the breakfast table."

I looked at him quickly but, if he noticed my response or found that proof of anything, he certainly didn't mention it.

"Admirable," he continued. "Loyal. You are to her what Tino is to me."

"If you mean he's your sister from another mister, who'll begrudgingly let you do his makeup and curl his hair, then yes, I am to her what Tino is to you."

He looked like he was attempting to repress a smile, and failing. "I stand by my statement."

"Nice to know you're comfortable in your sexuality, Mav."

He shrugged. "I will try anything once."

Jesus. I did not need to know that.

I mean, I liked knowing it. But knowing it was dangerous because I wanted to put that to the test and see exactly what he still had left to try.

"We thought perhaps you had eaten too many and fallen into a food coma," Antonio's voice heralded them arriving beside us.

Saved by the campana.

"No," I said with a warm smile as I shifted to make better space for him next to me. "But I did dribble juice all down my front. I considered washing it out, but thought a stain was more dignified than a wet t-shirt competition entry."

"I think there's a lot to be said about healthy competition," Antonio joked, and Olive and I laughed.

I snuck a look to Mav as Olive said something to Antonio and was pretty sure he was fuming. I had many thoughts and feelings about what exactly he might be fuming over. Was he annoyed we were interrupted? Did he not like the idea of me entering a wet t-shirt competition? Was he even less impressed by the idea that Antonio might be involved in said wet t-shirt competition?

It wasn't like my dress would be able to go all wet t-shirt competition entry on me anyway, there was far too much lining and structure going on. Part of me wanted to reassure Mav – if that was indeed the cause for his extra deep scowl – of that, and the other part wanted him to stew in jealousy and possessiveness because I got perverse pleasure out of it.

"I think it's about time for some dessert," I said. "Tino, come and feed me some chocolate covered strawberries."

He smiled as he hopped up and held his hands out to help me up. "You haven't sickened yourself of strawberries?"

I shook my head. "Never. I could *live* off strawberries."

I put my arm through his and we led the way back to the picnic blanket.

By the time we got back to the palazzo, I was very close to not wanting to see a strawberry ever again in my life. Only close, though. And despite all four of us having eaten what felt like our weight in food, we were still very ready for dinner.

If I kept eating like this, then I was going to have to do even more shopping.

CHAPTER SEVEN

The next week, Mav was clearly in wooing mode.

We trailed around vineyards like we had any idea about wine except how to drink it in vast quantities. Had perfumes made specially for us, and we pretended we were helping and making decisions. Ate at the most expensive places. Were flown to the mainland for more shopping and eating. Nightclubs. Extravagant parties with the crème de la crème. Horse riding. We were taken on tours of old castles, monuments, the piazza, and a gorgeous little church that were all steeped in history.

I was up at the arsecrack of morning, and I wasn't falling into bed until the wee hours of the next morning.

Yep, Mav was pulling out all the stops.

And, if he'd even for one second looked like he might have been enjoying himself, then maybe Olive could have fallen for it. As it was, she was just falling more and more in love with the country, the island, the people, the culture.

I mean, convenient for someone who was pretty much stuck here now.

Even if, by some miraculous twist of fate, she didn't have to marry Mav, she'd probably never want to leave.

Not that I wasn't also falling in love with everything as well.

It was like everywhere we went there was something beautiful and exciting to discover. The fact that Antonio seemed to feel it too, despite being native, made it all the more charming, and a place I could see myself not getting bored with all that quickly. Living here, under any circumstances, would hardly be the worst thing in the world.

Considering the purpose of the 'dates' was for Mav and Olive to fall in love – I assumed – Antonio and I hung back and entertained each other as much as possible. We bonded over the stupidest stuff. Most of it incidental and situation-based, and many jokes at Mav's expense. Mav's reply was, usually, a scowl and nothing more. Which earned him another joke at his expense.

A week later, however, the date was far more simple.

The beach.

Olive came hurrying into my room in excitement, her arms full of bikinis, and chattering about where we'd packed the sunscreen.

I blinked as I sat up in bed. "What are you on about?"

"Beach!" was her answer.

I blinked again. "Sand? Pass," I said as I flopped back onto my pillows. I got a pile of bikinis dumped on me.

"Half-naked guys. Wet. Athletic. Sexy," was her argument and I sat back up again in interest. She smiled. "I thought that would work."

"Is this your idea or…?"

She gave me a look over her sorting through her haul. "Mav planned it."

I nodded. "Right. So, another of your 'dates', then?"

Her smile grew rueful. "Like you haven't been enjoying them."

"Oh, no," I agreed as I crossed my legs and picked up a bikini top. "I'm loving them. All the benefits of being wooed by Mikhail Vitali without actually having to be the one unlucky enough to have to marry him."

Olive snorted. "You like him."

I scoffed. "I hate him."

She grinned at me as she picked up a two-piece and went to my mirror. "You'd sleep with him."

I opened my mouth to argue, and her eyebrow rose over her shoulder. I snapped my mouth shut and shrugged. "I'm only human," I reminded her.

"I'm human," she said pointedly. "But Mav's sort has never been my type."

"Why do you say that like it's always been *mine*?"

She smiled. "Because his sort *has* always been your type."

I couldn't argue with that. "Fine. In another life, I'd fuck him. But let's not pretend that Antonio isn't right up your alley."

She threw me a look. "I wasn't."

That made me ever so slightly better about lusting after her future fiancé.

"Oh, girl," I laughed.

We chose our bikinis and did the dutiful thing of covering up with not just beach dresses, but plenty of sunscreen too. Although, the idea of a beach dress always amused me because they were almost always made of sheer material or weirdly crochet-style design.

My version of a coverup was a long white shirt, but Olive's was a vibrant pink maxi dress thing with three-quarter sleeves and a full, a-line, skirt. It was stunning and just a tad extra. She looked amazing.

Armed with hats with giant brims, and huge totes full of things we probably wouldn't touch, we headed downstairs. As far as we knew, the plan was for one of the boys to drive us.

We found them waiting for us by a gorgeous little Aston Martin DBS convertible in dark blue, with the top down. I was taken enough by the car, then I was distracted by the guys.

Honestly, it seemed far-fetched enough that Olive and I had become surrounded by hot men. But then those sexy men had to go and be ready for the beach as well. I would say one good thing for Europe – out of ALL the good things – and that was the fact that they favoured tight, short boardshorts. There were also a lot of Speedos, but then it would hardly be fair on the rest of the world if the Continent was perfect.

Antonio wore a Baroque design shorts and button polo. The creams and browns complimented him well, and I wondered if these mobsters had fashion advisors or if they secretly just *really* cared about making sure they always looked impeccable and fashionable.

Mav would stand out less, but the whole image was no less because of it. His trunks were charcoal, and his shirt was thickly striped charcoal and white. It was, of course, unbuttoned. Which meant not only were impressive legs on full show, but also a body that may as well have been carved out of stone.

Sure, it made me drool a little, and I definitely wanted to know what he was packing under those trunks, but also, cliched much, Maverick? I mean, come on. Then, I suppose, if part of my job description was kidnap, torture, and murder, I'd probably be required and/or prefer to keep my body in top physical condition.

"Girls in the back?" Olive asked in the exact sort of excitedly vapid tone that I was sure gave Mav the impression she didn't have a lot going on under the perfect exterior.

It was as much as defence mechanism as just she was a naturally happy and bubbly person, which baffled me on a daily basis. Where I was always looking for the storm clouds, she was looking for rainbows. It was one of the infinite reasons we were perfect for each other.

Yin and yang, indeed.

In contrast to the picnic 'date', the beach 'date' was far more relaxed. The picnic had been enjoyable but felt like a stilted, modern version of a picnic out of a Jane Austen story. The beach, on the other hand, was all sun and fun.

Maybe it was because we'd spent the week exclusively hanging out together. The comfort-level had increased, the awkwardness dissipated, we knew each other better. Maybe it was just because we were all about to be half-naked and, really, how formal and proper can you be half-naked?

The four of us trooped onto the beach and hunted down a good spot. But no public beach for us. No. We weren't weaving in amongst sprawled bodies and belongings trying to find a patch of sand that would fit all of us. The whole beach was at our disposal. There was even a private bar which I had no doubt had chilled and frozen things enough to feed an army, and hopefully eats as well.

"What looks like a good spot?" I asked Olive, as though there were little offerings.

"Lounges or sand?" she asked me. We both knew what the other one's preference would be.

"I don't know why you bother asking," I said with a wry smirk.

"Why don't you either be selfish or take pity on your poor, unfortunate best friend."

Olive rolled her eyes, looked to Antonio like she thought he had any chance of making me be serious, then looked at me in fond exasperation. "Lounges it is."

I grinned. "Works every time."

"The only poor, unfortunate thing about you is your height," was Olive's cheeky response and I was *so* proud of her. She didn't usually tease me like that in front of other people.

There was a weird noise from the direction of Mav, and we all turned to look at him. He looked like he'd just snorted something fizzy out of his nose with red eyes and a slightly pained expression around his mouth.

"Are you okay?" I asked him.

He nodded toward Olive. "*Bene. È stato molto buono.*"

Even Antonio clapped in her direction, and she did a little curtsey.

I narrowed my eyes at them. "You watch who you're all calling short," I told them all. "You watch. I'm the odd one out. Maybe I'm the protagonist in this story? Huh?"

Olive smiled and kissed me cheek as she passed me. "You're the protagonist of my story, Coco."

God, I loved her.

"Fine. I forgive you."

Olive and I claimed a lounge, dropping our bags beside them and then beginning the shucking process. If it wasn't already obvious to the likes of Mav and Antonio that Olive and I were two very different people, the way we undressed would have been a dead giveaway.

Olive was there, gently disrobing, slowly and carefully, folding her dress and laying it in her bag to keep it clean and dry. Then there was me who, in one motion, dragged my shirt up over my head and threw in haphazardly onto the lounge, full-well knowing that I would get wet and sandy and then not move it when I lay down.

Present Me creating problems for Future Me once again.

After a quick scan of the vista – which was breathtaking, of course – I turned, and the vista was breathtaking in a whole different way.

Mav and Antonio had removed their shirts and were talking quietly enough between each other that I didn't hear the words, but they were both smiling. It was a carefree, unguarded moment between the two men, and it was very nearly enough to keep me distracted from their bodies.

I saw no tan lines and did wonder if the colour was either fake or if the guys ever indulged in a little nude sunbathing. The second image was, obviously, far more enticing.

So, it was everything that Olive had promised me – half naked men, wet (hopefully), athletic, sexy – but it wasn't a beach-full. It was only two. One of whom I could hardly keep my eyes off, but I knew I needed to. For my sanity. For Olive's.

Do not complicate things anymore than they have to be.

Except, then his eyes slid to me and it became painfully obvious that he also couldn't keep his eyes off me. Molten heat, in shades of the brightest grey-green, threatened to drown me. It was like one half of his brain was completely focused on the conversation with Antonio, but the other was all about me.

It felt good. I shouldn't have let it, but it did.

"Tino," I said loudly, and he turned to me. "Last one to the water's bad in bed!" And I took off running.

I heard Antonio cry out and then knew he was following. Now, I wasn't a slow runner. I was fit enough, used to walking and the occasional run. Certainly fit enough for a short sprint to the water and I should have given myself enough of a head start that I'd win.

Antonio's legs were longer and he managed to overtake me and hit the water just before me. He threw his hands up as he laughed in victory.

"You suck!" I laughed as I kicked water at him.

"I believe, by the terms of our wager, you suck," he countered.

I smirked. "Maybe I don't and that's why I'm bad in bed?" I suggested.

He threw his head back and laughed, clear and bright. The guy was, objectively, gorgeous. Sure, his physical features were great, but his personality was near perfection. He was bright, sarcastic, and had a wicked and eclectic sense of humour. We were two peas in a pod. He was just a thousand times happier and friendlier than me. He would have been a perfectly good Summer fling.

But he wasn't the one I wanted, and he was, as we'd said only that morning, much more Olive's type than mine.

I was thankfully distracted by Antonio picking me up over his shoulder and swinging me around. I laughed as he waded further into the water, then threw me in.

As I pulled myself back out of the water – with the autopilot check that all the right bits were still in my bikini – I pointed my finger at him.

"Oh, you are in for it now," I warned him.

We half-heartedly chased each other around, until I realised the bar had balls and I decided he needed a crash course in what the non-

European's called football. Why they had one, I didn't know. But I was going to make full use of it. I had to. I could feel Mav's eyes and me and it was taking all of my not very significant willpower to not just stare right back at him.

And, after a while, I still knew that Mav was enjoying the view as much as I was, but I was also having a great time. Olive and I sipped huge colourful, alcohol-filled drinks with real fruit and umbrellas. We walked through the shallows of the water like we were in some dramatic movie montage. We diligently reapplied our sunscreen at regular intervals because no one wants to wake up the next day and be redder than a perfectly ripe tomato and at serious risk of peeling just like one, too.

As a rule, I wasn't someone who enjoyed the beach. Sand got places it was not supposed to go. Salt stuck to you and made you feel weirdly sticky. It was horrifically hot. It was crowded. You got sand in your drinks. You lost your bather bottoms up your arse. You name it. Too many things to go wrong at the beach.

But that day was perfect. Absolutely perfect.

Sure, sand got places it wasn't supposed to be, but I just washed it off or ignored it.

Salt made me feel sticky, but it didn't bother me and I knew I could just shower when we got back.

It was hot, but it was the goddamned beach after all. It would have been even worse if it was cold.

Our drinks were wonderfully protected at the bar and just refilled if they got sand in them.

My bather bottoms made a break up my arse with gusto and often, but I just sorted them back out and was gratefully it wasn't a nip-slip.

When we got too hot and we were waiting for lunch, Mav had the bar people bring shades out for us to relax on the lounges.

It was the most opulent, luxurious day. We'd enjoyed more luxury that week, for sure, but there was something about such a simple experience being permeated by the wealth and lavishness of the Vitalis' lifestyle.

"I have never seen you this happy at the beach before," Olive pointed out and I smiled at her.

"You don't like the beach?" Antonio asked.

"Not as a rule," I told him.

Antonio laughed.

"What?" I asked him.

He shook his head. "No. It would just be a shame if someone had picked the beach as an outing for your love of nature."

"Aw," I said. "Did you think grass and sand were the same, Tino?"

He laughed again. "I didn't see the difference. Sand is better, no?"

"No," I said, like I agreed even though it was a contradiction.

Mav got up, took hold of the side of Antonio's lounge and tipped him off it. Antonio looked up at Mav with a humoured expression on his face, like there was some secret or joke between them that we weren't privy to.

"*I*," Antonio said with a laugh, "won't make that mistake again."

"Good," Mav said, looking like he was fighting a smile.

Honestly, the two of them were just like me and Olive. Fighting and bickering like siblings, but held together with a rock-solid love and loyalty, firm in the knowledge that any fight they had would only cause a temporary and minor rift, if that.

It was a beautiful thing to see in anyone, least of all in two men I'd ignorantly believed lived a life that wouldn't look kindly on such displays of affection with another person. Yeah, I guess they were killers and drug lords and weapons runners and whatever else they might have their fingers in, but they were people, too.

Because that helped me tame the way I felt about Mav, for sure.

CHAPTER EIGHT

The rest of the day was good.

After lunch, I forced myself to push Mav out of my head for long enough that I got lost in hanging out with Antonio while Mav and Olive talked – or didn't.

We chased each other around, trying to push each other over or get the other in a head lock for no reason other than we could. We made sandcastles. I buried his legs and made him a mermaid. He buried my legs and made me a crab – his artistic flare just proving how much more Olive's type he was. We bobbed around in the water and talked.

We even played pirates for a while, which mainly involved swordfights with things we pilfered from the bar. Mav and Olive even joined us – girls v guys of course – but, when it became woefully clear that Olive and were not the master swordswomen we'd led ourselves to believe, we switched to playing frisbee which at least all of us were fairly useless at.

It was late in the afternoon when we trooped back into the palazzo to get ready for Rico's little party. By all accounts, it was just an excuse for everyone to dress up a bit and have a more relaxed dinner and far too much to drink. I wasn't complaining. After having such an epic day of fun and sun, I was actually really looking forward to soaking in the bath, putting on a nice dress, and just hanging out with people who were becoming good acquaintance, if not quite friends.

Olive and I walked out to the terrace and I was still on a high. It was like nothing was going to bring my mood down. Even Mav's scowl from across the room didn't put a dent in it.

"I wonder what he's all grumpy about now?" I asked Olive.

"Probably how often Antonio had his hands on you today," was her response.

Did I notice a hint of jealousy in her voice? "Tino and I are just friends," I reminded her.

"I didn't say you weren't."

"Oh, so you believe I'm not into Tino, but still think I want to shag your future husband?" I teased.

She nodded. "Um, yes. Because there is absolutely no sexual spark between you and Tino, but you and Maverick cannot keep your eyes off each other like you're undressing each other whenever you're in the same vicinity."

"I'm not going to sleep with him."

"Not going to and wanting to are very different things, Coco," she said matter-of-factly as she smiled at Rico, who was coming towards us.

"You both look lovely," he said, his eyes not leaving her.

If I didn't know any better, I'd say that Rico was half thinking about just marrying Olive himself. It made me wonder who Mav's mum was and where she was. I couldn't remember Daniel ever telling me anything about her. She'd just never been mentioned, like the Vitali kids were immaculate – what? Ejaculate? – and I hadn't noticed until just then.

"It pleases me to hear you are spending more time with Maverick, Olive," he said warmly.

She nodded. "We're getting to know each other quite well, I think."

"*Bene*. Good. And you, Echo?" he finally turned to me. "You and Antonio are causing trouble I understand?"

I smiled as politely as possible. "Something like that, yes."

"Wonderful." Enough attention had been wasted on me. "Olive, shall we go and see if another drink will lift my son's frown?"

"Of course," Olive said prettily.

I gave her a smile and watched them walk away.

I could see Olive was really trying. She was trying to get to know Mav. Trying to give this future relationship a real go. She was doing her duty and she'd been damned if she didn't do it well. I was proud of her and I loved her, and I wanted only ever good things for her. I was just worried – in general, but particularly because of the daggers Mav was shooting me while he was shooting a tumbler of amber liquid – that her dance partner wasn't going to play ball.

"Have you had much time for dancing, Echo?" Antonio asked, appearing at my elbow.

I looked at him with a smile, forgetting Mav's frown for a moment. "Dancing? Not more than you've seen this week. I don't seem to have had time for anything much."

"Except getting lost," he teased, and I nodded.

"I do it so well," I responded, and his eyes shone.

"Can I entice you now?"

I shrugged. "Why not? Although, I warn you, if you wanna get fancy on the steps, I may not keep up."

"I will teach you, no?"

I smiled. "Sounds good."

So, among our little private soiree, Antonio taught me to dance. Well, he gallantly tried. Rico then took to the floor with Olive, and the two of them were sublime. They outshone Antonio and I. We stopped to appreciate them, but then my eyes wandered, and I noticed Mav was gone. I shrugged it off, and went back to enjoying the spectacle.

I slipped away to my room a little earlier than the others, but I was only alone for as long as it took me to get changed into my pjs and drop my tired arse onto the bed.

I heard a noise at my door and turned to see Olive sliding into my room, tears streaking her face. I was off the bed in an instant.

"What did he do?" I asked, because there was only one reason she was crying.

She shook her head, her hand to her mouth. "He's just so…" She shook her head again.

"Did he hurt you?"

Another shake.

I tried to decode the situation based on my knowledge of her. "Was he rude to you?"

Nothing.

"Dismissive? Generally, just a disrespectful arsehole?" That sounded like him.

She hesitated and it was enough to be a yes. She was putting on a good show for the others; the dutiful future fiancée, all smiles and warmth and vapid brainlessness. But I knew what shouldering all the effort was costing her. Because Mav sure as shit wasn't giving anything back. He was going through the motions because he had to, but he knew as well as us that there was no need for love. Even coming here and not expecting love, she must be finding his apathy trying.

Well, apathy this, dipshit.

"I'mma fucking hurt him," I muttered as I stormed to the door.

"Echo–"

"No, Ollie. He's not going to get away with this. Stay here."

I kept right on storming until I got to Mav's room. I was prepared to storm on in there, but it was locked. So, I banged on the door until he opened it.

"Back for round two so–?"

I shut him up with a forceful push to his chest that had him take a couple of steps backwards in a hurry. But even taken by surprise, he looked at me with cocky amusement.

"Miss Sump–?"

I shoved him again, but he wasn't going to let that stand. All humour dropped from his face. He pushed me right back. Into the door so it closed with my body hard against it. His hand was on my throat, and he was standing close enough that I was suddenly viscerally aware that I'd unthinkingly stormed in there in my thin summer PJ hot shorts and cropped camisole.

"What exactly did you storm in here to berate me about now, Miss Sumpter?" he purred, his voice like ice as his lips brushed my ear.

And the things he was doing to my body. Holy hells. It took me far too long to remember what I was doing alone in his room very barely clothed in the middle of the night. My clit definitely had other ideas about what could happen now I was there, but I was going to force my larger brain to be in charge.

"Olive's just come to see me," I told him, feeling my throat bob against his hand.

He looked me over, his nose almost brushing mine. "What the two of you get up to behind closed doors is your business, Miss Sumpter."

I glared at him. "She was crying, *Mikhail*."

The hand at my throat tightened slightly. "And I suppose you blame me, *Echo*?" My name was said with as much disdain as I'd said his. "Or does it annoy you more when I call you my nymph?"

"You don't need to call me anything. But you will start showing Olive the respect she's due. The respect your family is after by making you marrying her."

Something flickered in his eyes. It looked like surprise but, it was so fleeting, I couldn't be sure. "Jealous, little nymph?"

Just the smallest amount. Maybe. "No."

Yeah, he didn't believe me either. So, I turned it back on him.

"The only person I saw today being jealous, is you," I told him.

He pressed his body further into me. "And exactly who am I jealous of?"

I shrugged nonchalantly. "You seemed pretty jealous of Antonio."

He growled and, damn, it was sexy. "The only reason I have to be jealous of Antonio is his freedom."

"What freedom?" I asked, legitimately surprised he hadn't just outright denied it.

"The freedom to touch you as he wants. The freedom to make you laugh. The freedom to be with you the way he should."

I didn't hear jealousy in his voice so much as longing. Those things he'd just described were the things Mav wanted to do with me, how he wanted to be with me. I felt the breath knocked out of me for a moment. I was astounded. I couldn't think. My mind was just blank. I was just a walking bundle of emotions fuelled by alcohol. And those emotions were already messy as hell.

So, "Tino and I are just friends," was what snuck out of my mouth in a breathy whisper.

His lips brushed mine as he said quietly but forcefully, "You are your own woman. Who you are or are not with is your choice. But it does not make me want you any less. It doesn't mean that after a whole day of watching you smile and laugh, and in nothing but a bikini, that I do not *crave* every part of you. Want to feel every part of you. Feel jealous of any person who can be their true self with you. I think you feel the same but, if you don't, tell me now and that will be the end of it. I will back off."

With nothing but emotions in my body to be making all the healthy decisions, all I could do was shake my head. "I can't tell you that."

For a moment, he seemed confused. Then I was confused. Like we'd both forgotten which negatives we'd put where and what we were actually saying.

To remove the confusion, I grabbed his face in my hands and kissed him hungrily. His response was instant. The hand on my throat slid around so he was more cupping my neck as our kiss deepened. His other hand glided firmly around my side to splay on my back so he was hugging me tightly, pressing my body into his and – God – he was so hard.

That surprised me for some reason, then I remembered what he'd said when he opened the door. I shoved against him, and he took a step back to look at me. We were both already breathing far too heavily.

"Wait…what did you mean 'round two'?" I asked him.

He smirked. "Are we pretending we owe each other anything?"

I wasn't sure how I felt about that. "So, you just had someone else in here? You were *just* fucking someone else in here?"

He cocked his head to the side in a very non-committal gesture. "Her mouth, yes."

Okay. Not so bad. Then I wondered why it was such a big deal, morally? He was right, we didn't owe each other anything.

"I've had a shower since," he said, as though that made it all better.

Weirdly, it did make it less bad.

We were both still breathing heavily, like we were one wrong – or maybe right – move away from just launching at each other and devouring each other whole. Sexually. I actually quite liked the sound of that.

As though we shared one mind, we both surged forward, and our lips met again. It was frenzied. Hands roamed unchecked. Noses bumped until we finally found our rhythm. His fingers were trailing over my stomach, and I put my hand on them. We both opened our eyes and I stared into his as I slid those finger down between my legs. We were too close for me to see his lips, but I felt the smirk on them and saw the humoured victory in his eyes.

He shoved me back into the door again and our kiss got scorchingly hot again in no time flat. His hand trailed more purposefully over my skin. Designed to tease, to tantalise. My arms went around his neck and my fingers played with his hair as our lips battled it out for a supremacy neither of us were planning to cede.

My clit throbbed and I ached to feel him in me in a way I'd never felt before. It's not like this was my first rodeo, and certainly not the first guy to tease me until I thought I'd combust. But Mav showed me the real meaning of combust. The real meaning of tease. His fingers skimmed so damned close, but just never quite gave me what I wanted.

Our bodies rocked together with the momentum of our kiss and there was far too much fabric between us. I reached down for the bottom hem of his shirt, and we got it off him. Jesus, but I didn't think I'd ever get sick of that body. I ran my hands over it as I looked at him, then we were kissing again, and we still weren't close enough.

Finally, I felt his hand cup my mound and my legs parted for him. I felt him smirk against my lips as he slid into my pj shorts. He seemed very pleased to find there was nothing else under there but me. And a very wet me it was. His finger slid through me easily, and he explored, testing my reactions, like he was trying to see what got the best response.

Then his finger slid into me and I couldn't help biting his lip against the wave of gratification that swept through me. The ache subsided to a dull throb that was almost ready to admit that it had been satisfied. Steadily, he thrust his finger as his thumb found my clit and I inhaled sharply.

I could feel the self-satisfied smugness coming off him in waves and wrapping around me. It all just added to the whole atmosphere, and I was completely lost in everything that Mav Vitali was. At that moment, he was the most perfect thing in the world. We were the most perfect. It was like two halves had been made whole and all was right in the world. Destiny was fulfilled. And I didn't even care how corny and ridiculous that sounded, because all I could feel was the steady, even beating of my heart and the tingles he was sending shooting through my body as he played it like a master.

As the pleasure mounted in me, my head lay back against the door and his lips trailed to my neck. I gripped his hair tighter and rocked my hips with his rhythm.

"Getting me off first seems awfully polite for a hate fuck," I panted as my body writhed happily against his.

I felt his smile on my neck. "Not polite. Practical."

"Oh? How so?"

His teeth dragged over my skin, and I felt the sharp sting ricochet in my nipples.

"Easier access," he growled just as he broke an orgasm over me in the most delicious of ways.

Both my arms wrapped around his neck, holding his head close to my body as I breathed through the aftershocks. His finger traced lazy circles over my clit, making my whole body shudder in satisfaction. I actually let out a breathy chuckle.

"Easier access?" I clarified.

He nodded as he ran his nose over my chest and collar. "The wetter you are, the less resistance to me."

I yanked on his hair and made him look up at me. "Oh, you think one orgasm gets you full access?" I asked, with a wry smirk. "Cute."

Heat and desire pooled in his eyes. He wasn't disappointed in my resistance – minimal and superficial as we both knew it was. Rather,

I got the impression I'd pleased him by not giving in and begging him to rip off my shorts and bury himself deep inside me. Which was definitely exactly what I wanted.

"Exactly how much is this going to cost me?" he asked cheekily.

"You wanna buy your way in?" I teased.

He ran his hand over my body. Hard. "We both want me inside you, little nymph. If it's a question of cost, tell me your price."

I dropped my lips to brush his. "It's as much about quality as quantity, *Maverick*. Ten bad ones could pay off the same as one good one."

"You enjoy challenging me, don't you?"

"You enjoy being challenged, don't you?"

"Only by you."

He took my full weight and carried me to his bed. He lay me down gently, his body following mine. God, the control this man had of his muscles was such a turn on.

When my back was on the bed, he looked at me with a heated warning in his eyes and I raised my eyebrows in question. His only answer was to drop his head to my chest and plant kisses along my burning skin. My back arched into him, and his hands gripped my hips tightly.

"God, Mav," I breathed.

His nose dragged over my skin as his lips made their way down my body. My nipples pulled tight and my stomach erupted in flutters. Heat pooled between my legs and I so hoped that was his final destination.

He did not disappoint. He paused when his nose was millimetres from my slit. He had the audacity to look up at me, his eyes full of cocky triumph and arrogant amusement. But just then, I didn't care. His fingers had been magic, I wanted to know if that mouth was as sinful as it liked to think it was.

Mav hooked a finger in the leg of my shorts and pulled it aside. The cool air hit the heat of my centre and the sensation made everything else feel heightened. His nose ran over my clit slowly, like he was breathing me in, and I closed my eyes and just let myself enjoy everything he was unleashing on me.

I felt his tongue next, just as slow and gently as his nose had been. From pussy to clit. My whole body shuddered, and one of my hands closed around his hair. From there, I stopped hyper-focussing on what he was doing and just how it felt, and holy hells.

It didn't take long for the delicious flutters and tingles and building pressure to twist so tightly that it could only be incredible once it broke. Again, Mav did not disappoint.

"*Dio mio*," I moaned as my orgasm reached proportions definitely requiring an epic trailer soundtrack. My hands fisted his sheets and my whole torso rose off the bed.

I felt his breath of a laugh against the heat of my skin, and it sent tingles of pleasure skittering through me, making me shiver again.

As I got my breath back, he kissed his way back up my body, pushing my singlet up under my breasts and nipping my stomach gently as he went. And still, I wanted more. I wanted to feel his fingers dig into my body as he thrust deep inside me. I wanted to feel him throb, to come undone for me. I wanted to be the one to shatter him.

But it would be more fun to draw it out. Make him work for it. I couldn't just totally give into him all at once, could I?

I put my foot on his chest and shook my head. He sat back on his heels and looked at me, heat and question in those beautiful grey-green eyes. Slowly, I sat up and he licked his lip as he watched me.

"That," I told him, "is as far as you go, *Mikhail*."

He leant over, his body pushing mine back down into the bed. He was, incidentally, nestled between my legs, but he wasn't making a play for getting inside me. He ran a hand tantalisingly up the outside of my right leg as his lips dropped to my neck.

"I don't need to be inside you to get what I want from you, *nympha*," he purred and my whole body arched into him.

His hand slid firmly up my body, coming to rest on my ribs under my breast.

"You will be begging for it long before me." Then he nipped my earlobe and pulled away from me, standing up to get dressed like he hadn't left me to melt into a little puddle of want in the middle of his bed.

I wanted to beg for it then. I very nearly did beg for it then. I was stronger than my lust.

I very gracefully extricated myself from the dishevelled mess my writhing had caused in his bed sheets, and headed for the door.

"Remember what I said," I told him.

"Which bit exactly, little nymph?" he asked sassily.

"About Olive. She deserves your respect, and you will give it to her."

I put my hand on his door knob, and his body crushed mine into the door. His cock was still rock-hard and dug into my arse.

"Let me guess?" he purred as his fingers slid between me and the door to tease my overly sensitive clit. "I give it to her, and you'll give *it* to me?"

I smirked at his teasing. "Maybe."

"That is your price?"

"You have no idea how sexy respecting my best friend would be," I moaned, more put on than even the delectable tingles he was eliciting in me were worth.

"Very well," he said as he kissed my neck. "You dictate the price, and I will pay. Whatever it is."

Shit. That was sexy. I had to tell my nipples to calm the fuck down because I very much wanted to tell him to just stick it in now and be done with it.

I arched my arse into his cock. "Whatever it is?"

I felt him nod. "I am at your mercy, *nympha*."

I tried not to smile at that. "That seems like a very dangerous power to give me over you, Mav," I said quietly.

"No more dangerous than the power you already hold."

Now it wasn't just my stomach fluttering but my heart. I took a deep breath and nodded. "Okay, then."

He spun me gently and pressed the most intense, slow, deep, meaningful kiss to my lips. When he pulled away, the only sign he was as affected as me was deep in his eyes.

"Good night, little nymph."

I bit my lip and nodded once. "Good night, Mav."

I slipped out of his room, hoping I didn't look exactly as sexed up as I felt.

It was only on my way back that I realised that I'd just gone and left Olive in my room and I'd been gone I didn't even know how long. But I needn't have worried – much. When I opened my bedroom door, I found her asleep on my bed.

I felt a little guilty that I'd gone to tell Mav off then ended up hooking up with him, but I also knew she wouldn't have made jokes about me wanting him if she was fully against it. Although, it would have been so much easier if she was against it because then I'd have a reason to control myself.

As it was, I didn't want to control myself, but I knew I'd have to if I wanted to avoid as much shit hitting the fan as possible later.

CHAPTER NINE

The next day, I was a real mature young woman and avoided Mav for as long as possible.

Olive and I had had a very short conversation when she woke. I'd told her that I hadn't been able to sleep very well after having a go at Mav – which was true – and let her think it was because he infuriated me, and she knew how I got when I was angry. So, she said she'd organise some breakfast to be sent up to my room and let me to sleep for a bit longer.

Then Olive and I had spent the morning in the village, and the afternoon exploring the huge expanse of the palazzo. It was old, parts of it closed off and not even used anymore. So, colour us very surprised indeed when we found a legit bowling alley in what looked like it might have been a ballroom – or similar – once upon a time.

"THEY HAVE A BOWLING ALLEY!" we both cried at the same time, then still in sync, followed up with, "Of course, they have a bowling alley."

"Who doesn't have a bowling alley in their palazzo?" I asked like it was the most natural thing in the world.

"The poor," Olive answered, like it was obvious.

As far as alleys went, it was two lanes, but that was more than enough for us to bring out a touch of the old competition. We were just far more used to Wii Bowling than we were hurling real actual bowling balls. Which may or may not have been to our advantage.

Olive's ball went wild, and she ended up knocking all the pins down.

"No!" she laughed in annoyance.

I threw my arms in the air in victory. "Yes!"

"Isn't that supposed to be the other way around?" I heard Antonio laugh.

I span around, my arms still in the air. But Antonio wasn't alone. Just seeing Mav in all his scowly glory made my mouth go dry, my heart thud heavily, and my whole body respond. I lowered my arms slowly and wrapped them over my stomach.

"Oh, we're playing 'Go, Go Bowling'," Olive said happily.

"Uh, we agreed it was called 'Bowlf'," I reminded her, my insta-lust for Mav temporarily forgotten.

"No one's going to know what 'Bowlf' is," was Olive's favourite argument.

"Yeah because yours doesn't sound like a broken record with a creepy suggestion for a lame date," I retorted and I saw the smile in her eyes.

"Go, go bowling," Antonio whispered in a weird creepy, horror movie voice and a shiver actually ran up my spine.

"Argh," I chuckled as I hurried to Olive's side. "No."

He smiled. "Okay. I won't. *If* you let us join whatever it's called."

"Bowlf," I said as Olive said, "Go, Go Bowling!"

Antonio's smile widened. "Teams?"

"Fine," I said. "Any excuse to kick your butt."

He walked towards me. "Oh, definitely. But, fair's fair, Echo. I get Olive."

My eyes darted to Mav and my heart thudded harder. It was bad enough being in a room with him after the night before, but being on a team with him? Jesus. But no one could know that anything had happened between us, so I had to play it cool.

"Fine," I said, forcing the joviality. "But if he makes me lose, I'm blaming you, Tino."

He nodded. "It's a deal. Now." He clapped his hands. "What are the rules?"

"It's bowling, but with golf scoring. Whoever gets the lowest score, wins."

Antonio looked at me like I might have actually, legitimately lost my mind. I certainly felt like it. Maybe I had and I was just the last one to notice.

"What stops me just putting it in the gutter every time?" Antonio asked as he took off his jacket and rolled up his sleeves.

"The scoring rule," I said.

"There is a scoring rule?" Mav asked, his voice all deep and dark deliciousness.

God, one hook up and I was a mess of lust and hormones.

I tried not glaring at him, then changed my mind and let him have it. "There are always rules to…scoring," I said pointedly, hoping he realised I was referring to two kinds of scoring.

"You have to score at least a one on every shot," Olive explained, seemingly completely oblivious to the tension between us.

"And what if I'm just shit?" Antonio asked, picking up a ball like he knew exactly what he was doing.

"Honour system," I said. "You do your best to score one and, if you don't, you're buying."

Antonio nodded. "Okay. I can work with this."

"Whose turn is it?" Mav asked.

"I'd offer to start again, but I don't know how to do that on the machine," Olive said.

She was giving nothing away about her moment from the night before. Not that she should, and maybe it was just one of those times that you need to just vent a little, then you feel better, or at least can deal with whatever it is a little better.

Mav's eyes darted to me, then he nodded to her. "Here, I'll show you."

Olive smiled at him. "Thanks."

Antonio came over to me, his ball under his arm. "So, how much trouble am I in?" he asked.

I smirked at his competitive side. "You want to know if Olive's better than me or not?"

He looked at me winningly. "Help a guy out here, Echo," he begged.

I laughed and shook my head. "Oh, no. You want to beat me, you've got to do it with whatever handicaps you do or don't have." I shrugged. "That's just the way it is."

"Come on…" he pled.

I shook my head. "Nope. Sorry."

"Olive?" he called to her.

She looked over her shoulder from where she and Mav were fiddling with the scoring machine. "Yeah?"

"Are you better or worse than Echo?"

Olive looked at me and I felt like she knew my stance on

answering him. "I guess you'll just have to find out, won't you?"

"That is hardly fair," he laughed.

Olive shrugged, like she knew she should be sorry but definitely wasn't. "That's what you get for wanting to beat Echo."

"You're not even going to believe you're better than her?"

"I could," she agreed. "But watching you sweat it out is more fun than the slight bruising to my ego."

Antonio nodded. "All right, then. Game on."

Mav looked me dead in the eye. "Game on." The 'little nymph' was, obviously, heavily implied and I would have been surprised to discover the others hadn't heard it as well.

Mav and Olive had set it up for me to go first and I frowned. "Of course you did," I said, then looked at the screen. "Wait, which lane?"

"One," Olive said. "It was easier."

I nodded and took my place, hoping to all hopes that the goosebumps flaring to life across my whole body under Mav's watchful gaze weren't going to be too distracting from my game that was already suffering a little bit.

I loosed the ball and hit one pin. "Yes!" I cried as I spun with my arms up.

On my way back to the seats, I did a very arrogant strut that had Olive and Antonio laughing. Even Mav smiled and I let him have a small smile in response. Part of me knew that giving him anything was dangerous, but goddamn, I couldn't help it. There was another part of me that wanted to give him everything.

On my second ball, I followed the same line as my first and 'oh, no' accidentally didn't hit a single pin.

"Oh, no!" I cried sarcastically as I exchanged places with

Antonio,

"We'll see who is 'oh, no' soon, Miss Sumpter."

"Bring it, *Signore* Calabrese," I dared him.

Just as he was swinging through, I yelled out, "Antonio!" He let go at the absolute wrong moment, and knocked down four pins.

"Oops," I said and he turned a smirk on me.

"Is that how you're going to play it?"

I nodded. "That is how I'm going to play it."

"Coco, play nice," Olive chastised warmly.

I shrugged. "Can't. Tino just brings out the challenger in me."

"The cheater, more like," Olive said.

And it was indeed game on from there. From all of us, except Mav who was quietly doing his own thing and letting us do ours. I had the sinking feeling that he was plotting, which put me on edge. Every minute, I was waiting for him to do something.

I didn't know if it was going to cost me the game, or give away what had happened the night before. All it did was serve to make me a little hyper and full of excess energy that had to go somewhere. So it went into trying to put Antonio and Olive off.

I lowered myself to singing loudly and off-key – not difficult for my skill level. But they just joined in, louder and totally in key which ruined the whole thing.

I tried cartwheels across the lanes. That ended badly for me. Unsurprisingly.

I surreptitiously swapped all their balls out. And failed to notice they were doing the same to me.

Anything that didn't involve me and Mav in direct vicinity, I was up for. Which had me hovering around the others as they took their turns. Luckily, that was just generally off-putting enough that I didn't have to resort to physically touching them and being guilty of actual interference.

That didn't mean that Mav didn't corner me at the earliest opportunity.

As Olive and Antonio were locked in discussion regarding whether Antonio's gutter balls were on purpose or not, Mav appeared at my side and teased a caress over my stomach. Flutters burst to life and my fingers itched to touch him back.

"Honour system, huh?" he asked.

"What are you doing?" I hissed at him.

He bent his lips to my ear. "Doing my best to…score," he said, pretending he wasn't sure if he'd used the right word.

I turned my face to look up at him. "What do you want from me?"

"Your body, little nymph. Preferably writhing in pleasure under mine."

"And if I like it on top?" I countered.

He cracked a smile for a split second before dragging his tongue over his bottom lip. "Then perhaps it will be me writhing in pleasure, no?"

I heated and snuck a look to Olive while I collected my thoughts.

"Give in to it, my little nymph," he begged.

"I thought I'd be begging before you?" I sassed.

"I can admit when I'm wrong."

"You're supposed to marry the girls like Olive," I reminded him, as though that had any bearing on our conversation.

"*Si*, but I corrupt the girls like you."

Oh, why did I so much like the sound of that? Rude, is what it was.

My eyes flew back to his. "Corrupt me? That's your goal, here?"

"I am *il diavolo*, little nymph," Mav purred, and I wondered how much of that was a nickname and how much was purely designed to be enticing. "My *only* goal is to entirely corrupt you."

Consider me well and truly enticed. "Bold of you to assume there's anything pure left in me."

Humour danced in his eyes. "You are not as dark as you think you are. I will find your light, and I will make it mine."

Yes, please.

"Coco, your turn," Olive called happily and I pushed past Mav towards them.

"Come, Echo," Antonio said with a wide smile. "If I'm reading this correctly, it looks as though your score is higher than my score."

I glared at him, full of mock fury. "We're still in it." I threw a look back to Mav as I picked up my ball. "Besides, I'm hardly the weakest link in here."

Mav shrugged. "First time jitters," was his explanation.

Antonio and Olive found him unbelievably charming, I'm sure. I saw his little ruse for what it was. The guy liked to push my buttons, and he was going to find and push every single last one until I imploded. I'd be mad about it, but I'd enjoy it.

Things only got worse from there and it wasn't long before Antonio and Olive were celebrating resounding victory. I was busy glaring at the scores. Mav's in particular, that seemed to get worse with every shot. Had we been playing real bowling scoring, with those scores he'd have been the runaway winner.

Mav shrugged while I glared at him in annoyance. "It seems we are buying, no?"

I shook my head. "There's no we. *You're* buying."

He inclined is head. "All right. Tomorrow night. The club. Drinks are on me."

"No way!" Olive squeaked as though we hadn't already been clubbing together the week before. "Really?"

"Really. And I expect you both to dance."

"Coco loves dancing," Olive said quickly and she got to share in my glare-a-thon.

"Does she?" Mav asked, turning a predatory look on me.

I swallowed hard and nodded. "Semi-naked bodies, sweaty and horny, fondling in the dark. What's not to love?"

Antonio clapped his hands together. "Wonderful. We celebrate tomorrow then."

"Tomorrow," I said, looking at Mav like it was a promise.

I wasn't exactly sure what the promise was, but I knew I was going to stick to it. And I knew he was looking forward to it.

CHAPTER TEN

If I was going to do this, I was going to do this properly. Even if I shouldn't.

I found my shortest, sparkliest, lowest cut dress. The skirt was clinging but short enough I still had plenty of movement, it was entirely backless, and required the sturdiest of body tape to makes sure my tits didn't pop out of it at every opportunity. I paired it with a pair of monster satin, chunky platform heels.

My hair was beachy waves, artfully messy in a way that would make Olive twitch to tame into perfect curls. My eyes were exaggerated and smoky, and my lips in nothing but gloss. If there was any risk of me hooking up – with anyone, not necessarily my best friend's future husband – then I didn't go in for coloured lips. Last thing I wanted was smeared lippy, and no 'long-stay' lipstick I'd ever tried had been true to its word.

Goddamn, but I looked good.

And I wasn't the only one who thought so.

"For once, you're dressed the part," Olive teased with a smile as I walked down the hallway towards her in one of the dresses we'd bought the week before.

I spun as I did, showing everything off. "Nightclub dress code is my jam. Low neck, short hem and make sure you sparkle, baby!"

She laughed as she took my arm in hers and we made our way downstairs.

"Mr Vitali and Mr Calabrese will meet you there," Corvi said as he opened the car door for Olive.

"Let me guess, they had business to attend to?" I asked over the car as Olive slid in.

Corvi closed her door and fixed me with a stare. "No trouble tonight, Miss Sumpter. Please."

I shrugged as I opened my own door. "It's not my fault if Maverick has a short fuse. He's *so* fussy about the weirdest things," I said as though 'wasn't that odd?'.

Corvi rolled his eyes but said no more.

He took us to the club, and I wondered why this was the first time Mav had brought us here. The last time we went out, it had been on the mainland. Maybe his club was one of those sordid, sex clubs. God, I hoped so.

As Corvi opened Olive's door, she took my hand and tugged me towards her door.

I gave her a nod and slid over to follow her out.

We were ushered straight in and to the VIP section upstairs. Trés original, but what did I know about nightclubs?

As soon as I stepped onto the top step and Olive had moved aside, my eyes met Mav's and I saw the hunger in his. It was very similar to the sudden hunger eating at me. Because this was Mav the way I'd seen him that night he'd taken away my cigarette.

His hair was ruffled out of its usual pristine slicked back style. He was in black jeans, with rips down them, and his shirt was a sheer and solid black stripe. Had someone told me a shirt like that existed,

I'd have said it would look ridiculous. It didn't look ridiculous on Mav. The tatts on his arm were stark under the strobing lights. And the hooded heat deep in his eyes was threatening to make me combust.

He was sitting in pride of place, in the middle of everyone, so there was no forgetting who the most important person in the club was. Men surrounded him, all with women hanging off them. All except him and Antonio. The guy to his left was actually in the middle of receiving a blow job, not that he seemed to be paying her much mind.

The men were all talking to him, but I didn't think he could hear them anymore. I certainly couldn't hear the music even thought I could feel it thumping deep in me. Or, that could have just been my heartbeat. Or, possibly even just the loud demands from my clit to let him have at us.

I watched as his eyes finally left my face and trailed ever so slowly down my body. And it just got me hotter. I had to check that that effect had been the lights and not literal sparks erupting between us. I felt like the energy zinging from him to me and back would be able to power this whole place for the next decade.

By the time his eyes had – painfully slowly – made their way back to mine, my whole body was flushed and I was biting my lip. Even more embarrassing, I was pressing my thighs together like that was actually going to ease the ache that pulsed there, like it was beating out his name.

Mav Vitali.

Mav Vitali.

Boy, this might have been a bad idea.

Ignoring those around him, he stood up and walked over to Olive and me. I realised Antonio was already talking to Olive while I had completely forgotten the rest of the world existed outside Maverick fucking Vitali. Ever dutiful, Mav said hello to Olive first, then turned to me.

Under the guise of polite greeting, Mav laid his hand on the lowest point of my back and leant his lip to my ear as he kissed my cheek. "I didn't know you could be more irresistible, little nymph"

I felt my cheeks heat and was glad for the dark, strobing lighting. "I am more than just my looks, Maverick."

I felt him nod. "*Si*, but your mind, you give me. Your body, I have barely begun to taste."

Flutters traitorously erupted again. Denying him was more about power than it was principle at that point. A power play that we both got off on.

The club in general was dark and busy. The VIP section even more so. No one was really paying any attention to anyone else. The perfect place for hands to roam where they shouldn't and not be easily caught. My fingers walked up his chest until I could hook one over to first button he had done up and tug him closer towards me. He didn't hesitate to drop his body down.

I let my lips graze his ear as I said, "And I suppose you think you're going to taste it tonight?"

I felt his groan rumble through his chest. "I believe there is still a price to pay."

I smiled. "You're still interested in paying it?"

He took my hand and brushed it over his crotch. "You will be the only one to ease my need, little nymph. I will pay your price until you so choose."

"And if I never choose?"

"Then I'm going to spend the rest of my life a very frustrated man." His hand slid between my legs. "But please, feel free to not choose. My father I'm sure, would appreciate my new focus."

"Because you're actually going to stop chasing tail and do your job?" I sassed.

He nuzzled his face against my neck. "Yours is the only body I want to touch. If you want. Yours is the only body I want touching mine. Again, if you want."

I sighed against him. "If I don't want?" Which was not a thing, but worth clarification.

"Then I think we will both be very frustrated, no?"

I smiled and bit my lip as I pulled away to look at him. "I believe you demanded we dance, *Signore* Vitali." I raised one eyebrow.

"Are you asking, Miss Sumpter?"

"I don't ask, Maverick. But I'll be on the dance floor…if you're worried about who else might touch me out there…" I left the insinuation hanging and headed down the stairs.

Olive was safely with Antonio and I really shouldn't have been encouraging Mav but, I guess Olive could hardly complain when she was very obviously flirting with Antonio, even if she hadn't actually noticed it was so overt.

I added an extra sway to my hips as I made my way back down the stairs, not difficult with the height of my heels, and made my way towards the throng of bodies on the dancefloor. I'd barely stepped into the crowd when I felt a hand in mine and looked back to see Mav there. The heat in his eyes was predatory again, it was a challenge, it was the rise to my challenge.

I tugged him into the bodies and ours were forced together as we started to dance.

His hands were hot on my hips. I wrapped my arms around his neck and enjoyed the fact we were closer to the same height than usual. Mav's lips dropped to my jaw, and I leant into him further. We ground together and every nerve in my body came alive to his touch. I felt drunk and I hadn't even touched alcohol that day. Mav was giving me that floaty, slightly disconnected but hyper fixed on certain things feeling. And Mav was the certain things.

When I was sure I was about to unzip him from his jeans on the middle of the dancefloor, I felt him take my hand and lead me back through the crowd. But we didn't head back up to the VIP section. He took me down a hallway filled with doors. It didn't take a genius to work out what those rooms were probably for.

He got to the end, to an obnoxiously gold door, and put his thumb on the door handle until it went green.

"Perks of being the boss?" I asked.

He threw me a smirk over his shoulder before he pushed the door open. Then he led me in before following and closing the door behind us. In one glance, I took the room in. There was a couch, a bed, a stripper pole, and a wall full of toys. The music playing in it was softer and there was no sound of the music outside.

"How many girls have you brought in here?" I sassed.

I felt his hands on my hips before he turned me back to face him. He picked me up and my legs wrapped around his waist.

"How much do you care?" he sassed right back.

"How many more will there be?" I asked and, yeah, I was testing him.

Sure, we'd known each other barely three weeks. But he had just claimed that I'd be the last woman to touch him and I wanted to know if he was serious about that. I didn't care how many women were in his past – as long as he'd been sensible – but I did care how many he saw in his future. I ignored any reason why that might be and just went with it.

"You will be the last," he promised.

My legs tightened around him, and our lips met.

"*Nympha*," he groaned against me.

"Mav?"

"Can I touch you?"

I felt myself smile and nipped his lip. Our eyes opened and met.

"You are touching me, Mav."

"You know what I mean."

I nodded. I did. "Touch me."

His hand slid up my body to gently squeeze my breast and I felt it in my clit. I leant my forehead to his and we stared into each other's eyes.

"Tell me where you want it."

"Do you mean where on my body, or are you hoping I'll beg to be strung up from the ceiling completely at your mercy?"

"While the imagery along makes my cock twitch, little nymph, I want to know what you want."

I bit my lip while I thought about it. We were here now, so may as well make use of it. As though I wasn't drenched and throbbing for his touch alone.

I patted the arm under my arse to signify him to put me down, and he lowered me gently to the floor. I grabbed the front of his shirt and pushed him into the couch before placing a knee on other side of his legs. He scrunched my skirt up around my hips and held them tightly as I sat down on him.

"Not exactly what I had in mind," he said softly as I rubbed wantonly against the raging boner in his jeans.

"What did you have in mind?" I asked him. "Tell me."

I dragged myself over him again and saw the spark of heat flicker hotter in his eyes.

"I've always been better with my hands than words, *nympha*."

I smirked. "Then show me."

He tugged the fabric of my dress from the tape across my breast and pulled it down to reveal my naked flesh. He took my nipple in his mouth and sucked hard. I arched against him and my fingers dug into him.

The hand that had pulled my dress down slid around my back to hold me tightly against him so there was no escape. The other slid between us and found my clit. But it wasn't slow and steady that he was aiming for. From the first touch, he unleashed a torrent of pleasure that had my body writhing and shaking as orgasm after orgasm wracked me. It was more like one long one that rose and fell depending on how much torture he was inclined to lavish upon me. And I loved every second of it.

My hand reached down between us and ran over the bulge in his pants and the war in me ignited. I pressed my forehead to his and he seemed to know now wasn't the time for more pleasure.

"Why are you fighting something two consenting adults want?" he asked me, kissing me gently.

He didn't sound accusing or spiteful. It was a genuine question. He just couldn't understand why, when I so clearly wanted this – him, us – I was putting up a fight. Sometimes, I didn't know why either. I didn't think it hurt to tell him when, at that moment, I did know.

I ran my fingers through his hair. "At the end of this Summer, you're supposed to propose to Olive. Then you'll be expected to marry her. The next logical step is children and I'm sure everyone involved will be expecting it to be natural conception. I get your people might be a little vague on the fidelity front, but I won't be anyone's mistress. And I can't…" I paused to choose my words. "I can't totally give into you now, knowing what the future holds. You and Olive might fall in love one day, and it would kill me to hate her for that. Kill me to know that I still wanted you and you were hers."

He looked me over carefully. "I will never love her, *nympha*."

I didn't know if I read into that that he could love me, of if he was actually implying that, but I wasn't going to go there now.

"But *she* might love *you*."

He nodded. "I understand."

And I was just selfish enough to take one step closer to damnation. Let it not be said that I didn't take stupid risks. I had always liked to play with fire.

I took his hand and directed it to my slit. I gasped as he rubbed me then took his face in my hands as I kissed him. Our kiss was deeper, less frantic. His finger pumped me with a slower, steadier pace. I rolled my hips in time with his rhythm, fucking his finger like we were making love.

I was so close, my walls were tightening on him. His other hand palmed my breast, then his fingers rolled my nipple and it was enough to send me over the edge. The fall was like slow-motion. A great big wave that crested in weighted glory, wrapping around me and spreading warmth through my whole body.

Mav thrust one, twice, three times more as I rode the aftershocks before he slowly slid out of me. He wrapped me up in his arms and kissed me deeply. I inadvertently rubbed against him, and the sensitivity sent another shockwave through me. But he was still rock hard. I was feeling like maybe he deserved a reprieve.

I pulled away from him gently and onto the floor to nestle between his legs. He watched, his hands by his sides, as I undid his jeans. The only time he moved was to help me pull them down enough to free his cock.

Keeping my eyes pinned to his, I slowly slid my mouth over him and I watched the satisfaction burn molten in him. As much as I knew he was eager for it, he did nothing more than let me go at my own pace. Now and then his eyes closed and he nearly leant his head back against the couch, but the he'd open them again to look at me.

I laced my fingers with his as my other hand went to his shaft, allowing me to work more of him. My blowjob game had never been overly criticised, but I had an awful gag reflex.

The state of my gag reflex was irrelevant though as we were interrupted by Antonio's voice.

"Scusami, sei necessario, capo."

I shot off the floor, hurrying to cover myself back up, and looked at May in horror, picturing all sorts of sordid things. He stood up and tucked himself back into his pants.

"Oh, my God. Are people watching?" I hissed at him as I struggled to straighten my skirt.

"*Nympha*," he started, taking a step toward me and I shook my head and stepped back.

"Don't you '*nympha*' me, Maverick," I told him firmly. "What the hell is this place?"

"My private room."

I nodded. "Right. And just how many tickets do you sell to your private room?"

"None. There's an intercom for emergencies. Antonio can reach me. There are no two-way mirrors or cameras or spy holes. It is soundproof. There are no microphones. It's just you and me."

"And Antonio's disembodied voice," I huffed, not sure if I should believe him.

A ghost of a smile danced at his lips, and he nodded. "And Antonio's disembodied voice," he agreed.

He stepped up to me and I didn't back away this time. I let him put his hands on my arms, trailing down them until he took both my hands in his.

"I will try anything once, little nymph, I have told you that. But the one thing I will not do is share you. Not even to put on a show. If that gets you off, you will have to find someone other than me for that."

I looked into his eyes, and I believed him. Finally, I nodded. "Okay, Mav. Okay. I…trust you."

He hugged me, pressing a kiss to my hair. "Thank you." It felt like he was thanking me for more than that.

"For what?"

"For choosing to touch me. I am sorry we were interrupted."

I bit my lip as I tried not to smile and seem like I was happy to forgive and forget so soon. "Well, maybe, if you're a very good boy, you'll get lucky again."

He gave me that full half-smirk. "I hope so, *nympha*. But that will be up to you. Now, I must go before Tino loses his shit. Go to the VIP lounge, Olive should be there, and I will meet you back there."

I nodded.

He pressed one more kiss to my lips, then ushered me out. Antonio was waiting for him in the hallway. If Tino thought it was weird that Mav was walking out of his private room with me, then he didn't say anything, he just gave me a smile and a nod. His expression was a bit tight, but I felt like that had more to do with whatever he needed Mav for than the situation he'd found us.

I gave him a nod in return, and hurried off to find Olive.

CHAPTER ELEVEN

The next morning, Olive's entry to my room was far less chipper than usual.

I didn't blame her. I barely remembered how or when we'd got home, only that Mav and Antonio had had to carry us up the stairs. Not a good look, but I didn't think we were horrendously messy, they were just being cautious. We'd spent the rest of the night drinking and dancing and I'd sworn to stay closer to Olive. Mav hadn't seemed to disagree with my choice.

Olive groaned deeply as she dropped onto my bed next to me and curled up on my other pillow. "I don't even remember my own name," she complained and I smiled.

"You certainly won't remember the name of the guy whose throat you had your tongue down, then," I said and her head flew off the pillow to glare at me in horror.

"What?"

I sniggered and she frowned.

"Not cool. I actually thought I might have got some action last night."

"I can't rule out that you did."

Her smile grew wry. "No. Where were you?"

I shrugged. "Nowhere."

"Getting your own action, more like." She shoved me playfully and I laughed.

"Maybe."

"Who?"

"I never kiss and tell."

"You *always* kiss and tell," she reminded me.

I nodded. "I give you the sordid details. I don't divulge names."

"Since when?"

"Since we're sophisticated society ladies."

"You've never wanted to be a sophisticated society lady."

I smiled. "I've started seeing the perks."

"You mean, the endless tabs. Waited on hand a foot. Private beaches. People to drive you wherever you want the minute you want it. People watching you with jealousy and intrigue?"

I nodded. "Something like that."

She laughed. "You've always had that, you've just literally never used it."

I nodded again. "I've started seeing the perks," was my excuse.

"Are the perks tall, dark and handsome who only smile when you're in a room and know they're the sexiest and most superior man whoever they're with?"

I scoffed. "No."

She nudged me and I looked at her with humour dancing across my lips.

"No!" I assured her, not feeling like I was lying. "Okay, I conceded that your future husband is the sexiest thing I have ever seen on two legs, but he's supposed to propose to you at the end of the summer, Ollie. That's just a recipe for all kinds of weird."

She leant her head on my shoulder. "I feel nothing for him except a small sense of amicability and, sometimes, outright vexation."

I snorted. "Doesn't mean it won't get messy."

"Coco, it's us. You can be honest with me."

I slid out from under her head and got up. "I am being honest with you!" I assured her. "Whatever you *think* you see between Mav and me… It's nothing. It doesn't change anything."

She sighed, watching me like she was looking for the bullshit. She didn't pull me up on it. I knew her well enough to know that she was most likely just dropping it because she knew I'd get cagier the more she pushed. I hoped she just believe me, but I wasn't that naïve.

Olive might have put on the sweet and innocent mask to the world and she might have even been that way about some things but, when it came to me, she was shrewder and more canny than Sherlock himself. And she knew it was just a matter of time before one of us was proven right. In this circumstance, it would be either the continued nothing between me and Mav, or a torrid love affair that she would do her best to assist.

I knew it was only a matter of time as well, and I hoped to anyone who might listen to a prayer that it would be me proved right.

"I guess we'd best go down to breakfast," she grumbled as she lay back on my pillows.

I shrugged. "I prescribe some hair of the dog."

She looked at me with a question. "What?"

I shrugged. "Let's just keep drinking?"

She was clearly thinking about it. After a second, she nodded. "Yeah, all right. Brunch?" She looked at the time on her watch. "Early brunch?"

I nodded. "Many would still call that breakfast," I pointed out. "But I like it."

We decided not to bug Corvi and have a day just to ourselves. So, we found ourselves one of the Vitali drivers and got them to take us down to the village and set about looking for what had become one of our favourite little cafes.

Breakfast included mimosas – we were pacing ourselves – then we thought a bit of window shopping was in order. Our plan was to find the most outrageous things that we would never in a million years buy because they were far too flamboyant.

When it was time for lunch, we went looking for the place that had become one of our favourites. Except we'd got ourselves completely turned around.

We went around a corner, and I looked around. "Hang on, I think it was the other way."

Olive nodded. "I think you're right."

We turned and made to retrace our steps.

"Oh, *scusami*," I said as I bumped into some guy coming around the corner.

He muttered something, and I paid him no more mind as we hunted down the little bar. We ate antipasti for lunch and drank wine as we sat on a deck overhanging the sea, and I felt like I'd stepped into some story book or something.

"This is insane," I said to Olive.

She smiled at me as she poured more wine. "What now?"

I shrugged. "We're sitting in this absolutely beautiful place, just eating and drinking and enjoying life with zero responsibilities. Like, what even is our life now?"

"You like this," she accused.

I shrugged. "Okay. Yes. I do. Is that a crime?" I laughed.

"No," she chuckled. "Not at all. I'm just... You've been so... Light this Summer, Coco. I don't know what it is about this place, but you're just..."

"Happy?" I suggested softly and she nodded. I looked around the deck and twiddled my wine stem in my fingers. "I haven't forgotten my past, Ollie. But here...I feel like I can start again. Does that make sense?" I scratched my head as I sat back in my chair with a huff of laughter. "I don't know. It wasn't a conscious decision, but that's how it feels. Like I can put it all behind me and just...be. My past is still part of me, but it doesn't cast quite such a big shadow anymore."

She reached over the table, and I took her hand. "It makes perfect sense. No one can tell you how you feel, or how you *should* feel. I'm just happy for you. If I didn't know better, I'd say there was someone to blame for it."

I squeezed her hand and pulled away again. "But you do know better."

She nodded, but I could tell she was just placating me. "I trust you to tell me your truth, Coco. Whatever that truth may be at any given time."

I looked at her shrewdly. "Are you going to give this up?"

She took a sip of her wine, shrugging her shoulders and kicking her eyebrows in a 'who knows?' gesture.

I had to laugh. "What about you and Antonio, then?" I asked and her cheeks actually heated. "NO?" I cried excitedly, leaning forward.

She shook her head as she swallowed her next sip. "Nothing's happened," she said.

"Then why the blush?"

There it went again, flaring across her nose in the cutest way. "What blush?"

I snorted. "Your face not on fire?"

She shook her head, looking like she was trying to hide behind her wine glass. "No."

"You like him," I teased, if anything to get her off the topic of me and Mav.

"He's nice." She shrugged.

"He's very nice, and you want to shag his brains out."

She snorted now. "Do I?"

I nodded. "Obviously. Why else the blush?"

"Oh, is that what your cheeks are doing every time you see Mav?"

Now my cheeks heated, and I cleared my throat. "What?"

"What?"

"What my cheeks are doing?" I clarified and she nodded.

"Yeah. I didn't realise that was you telling him you wanted him to shag your brains out."

I cleared my throat again. "I don't know what you're talking about."

She stuck her nose in her glass. "No, but Mav does."

After lunch, it was more wandering, just investigating the places we'd never stopped to look at properly or wanted to look at again. We took stupid photos and ate ice cream.

I looked back and there was an unpleasant tingle at the base of my head and in my stomach.

"What?" Olive asked, following my gaze.

I frowned, not seeing a reason for the sense of menace I was feeling. I shook my head like that would clear it. "No. Nothing. I don't know."

She smiled at me like she was hoping I was okay. "Are you going to hurl? Because I haven't seen your hurl for years."

I laughed, all dread now gone again. "No. I'm not going to hurl. In fact, I think I might be sobering up."

"Well," she said. "We can't have that."

I shook my head. "No. Where to?"

It was the best and laziest day. Just me and my best friend, no one else to watch us and judge us or berate us for being silly little girls. Later, we were at another bar and I got that feeling again.

My glass paused on the way to my lips and my eyes were scanning before I recognised the tell-tale feeling of threat again. Nothing obviously stood out, then I saw movement by the wall. A guy had been standing there and he was very conspicuously moving around now. I looked closer and realised I'd seen the guy before.

I'd seen the guy before a lot.

And nothing before this Summer.

Every time we were in the village, I'd seen him. By a doorway. Turning a corner. In the background of a shop. Coming around the corner just earlier that day. It was too many times to be a coincidence. He'd paid us too much attention to be a coincidence. Unlike all the other usuals we saw in the village, he's always had eyes on us.

My stomach got heavy, and I was worried I was going to hurl after all.

It wasn't us he'd been watching. It was Olive.

I looked at her, then looked around and wondered why we'd been stupid enough to leave the palazzo without Corvi. And I couldn't off the top of my head remember where we'd left the driver.

Think, Echo, think, I chastised myself. *Whose fucking brilliant idea had it been to be drunk all day?*

Oh yeah, mine.

I finished my drink as quickly as I could without bringing undue attention to us and kicked Olive's foot under the table. She looked at me with a smile.

"We should go," I told her.

She looked at me quizzically, then I saw she was about to look around the bar.

I kicked her harder and forced a smile. "Just act natural and follow me."

I waited until the table next to us, who'd been looking like they were going to leave for a few minutes, all stood up and paused while they continued their conversations, drawing out the time they'd have to part. I nodded to Olive, stood up and held my hand out for hers. She took it and I dragged her in a dignified duck to the door, hoping the crowd would cover us for long enough.

"Coco, what's going on?" she asked.

"Just keep up," I told her, my heart beating a mile a minute as I pulled my phone out of my pocket.

As I pulled up straight again, I ran into a body and my phone fell to the ground. Not looking at who I'd run into, I dropped to the ground to grab it. The body got there first, and I flinched as their hand bumped mine. Then I realised I recognised their scent better than I'd know my own.

I looked up into familiar grey-green eyes and comfort flooded me.

"What?" he asked, as though the fear and panic were written

clearly on my face.

I shook my head. "Not here," I whispered, reaching again for Olive's hand. "Where's your car?"

He pointed behind him. I gave him Olive's hand. "Do not let her go," I told him.

Instead of laughing or brushing my concerns off, he seemed to trust me. His eyes searched mine for the space of a single heartbeat before he nodded and led Olive back to his car. I followed them quickly, always with one eye over my shoulder, the other scanning for any other threats.

If Olive had a stalker, were they working alone? Was it just some native who'd seen her and got a bit creepy? Or was it part of something more sinister?

Daniel had prepared me for a lot, but he hadn't prepared me for this. Not really. But then, I didn't know how he'd have been able to. He'd had me trained in mixed martial arts for self-defence, but I was demonstration-level at best, used to sparring with people my own size. I hadn't got to anyone bigger yet. I'd been going through the motions, thinking that it would be enough to make us feel safe when a million miles from home. I'd been naïve about the realities and now Olive may very well pay the price.

Mav pulled the front seat forward so I could climb in the back, then helped Olive in. He jogged around the car and slid into the driver's seat. As he started the car, he caught my eye in the mirror and said, "Explain."

"Olive has a stalker," I said.

"What?" she squeaked.

Mav frowned as he pulled out of the park. "Who?"

"I don't know. I only just noticed. He's been following us nearly all Summer."

"You've only seen him here on the island?"

I thought back. "No. Once on the mainland last week, but not before we came here."

"Is he always alone?"

"I think so." I reached forward and took Olive's shoulder.

Mav swore colourfully. "Okay. There's only so much we can do without knowing more. Obviously, you two will not be allowed to leave the palazzo without more security."

I nodded. "I know," I said, responding to the actual accusation he was levelling. "That's on me. Never again."

He inclined his head, and I knew he believed me. He might think a few choice things about me as a person, but even he knew I would never endanger Olive on purpose.

CHAPTER TWELVE

With very little for Mav to go on, he said he'd take the whole stalker thing under advisement and make some enquiries.

Poor Olive had spent the trip back listening to me argue with him about him not trusting me.

"I trust you!" he'd shouted. "I trust you know when you're in danger. I just cannot do anything with 'he gave me a creepy feeling and he's been following us'. Do you remember what he looks like or if he was with anyone else?"

I'd had to shake my head and admit defeat on that one. I knew I'd recognise him again, even if was just by feeling, but he'd had one of those faces that are hard to picture in how generic they are.

Nothing seemed to come of it. Nothing was said by anyone else about any changes in behaviour or routine. And I started feeling like maybe I'd just overreacted about the whole thing. It wasn't like the guy had done anything, he'd just been there. It was quite possibly just a coincidence. He wouldn't have been the first person we'd seen more than once. It was inevitable on an island that small with only one main town.

So, by a few days later when we were bored and wanted something to do, Olive and I went down the hill again. This time, Mav and Corvi insisted on coming with us. In Mav's words, he wasn't letting us out of his sight. I knew he was hoping we'd see the guy again and then Mav would be able to see him as well.

This time, it was Mav who was not disappointed. Although I'm not sure that it helped.

Olive and I were wandering down a side street while Corvi and Mav talked a little way back – personally, I think Mav liked someone like-minded to not have to pay attention to us trying to decide if we needed more ice cream or not and I didn't blame him – and I was looking the total other direction when Olive suddenly squealed.

I spun and saw the guy was grabbing for her arm.

"MAV!" was the first thing out of my mouth as I stepped towards the guy.

I didn't know what I was going to do against him. He was probably over six feet of muscles on muscles, with great big scars marring his features. The number of them either spoke to the sheer volume of shit this guy saw, or he was a little useless at his job.

"Olive!" Mav yelled as he skidded to a stop at the end of the street, and Corvi was close behind.

The guy looked between me and Olive like he was confused for a second. He looked to Mav and Corvi and seemed to be judging how much time he had. He dropped Olive's arm and took a step towards me, reaching for something at his belt.

"Miss–?" he started.

Then there was a loud crack, a loud, "Oh my, God!" from Olive, and something whizzed between his face and mine.

A bullet lodged in the doorway to my left, but it wasn't going to deter the guy. He took another step towards me, and another bullet loosed. The guy tried to dodge it, but it clipped his arm, shearing a cut through his shirt.

I took a step back.

The guy seemed to know when he was shit out of luck and took off at a run.

"Stay with them," Mav barked at Corvi as he passed me.

"You could have hit me!" I snapped at him.

"No, I couldn't," he shouted back as he disappeared.

"Miss Carlione, are you all right?" Corvi asked as he fussed over Olive.

I took a step towards her, wanting to fuss over her too, make sure she was okay, shake the sense into her for not hitting him or kicking him or something. But my eyes kept slipping to where the guy and Mav had disappeared. For a moment, I thought I was worried about Mav, then I realised that wasn't it.

I didn't know what it was, but it niggled at me and I couldn't shake it, even as we were safe in the car on our way back to the palazzo with a resigned Corvi and an irate Mav.

He was more pissed that he'd lost the guy, I knew that. But he wasn't above taking it out on me, like it was my fault. He and Corvi were grunting more than talking to each other in rapid, broken Italian. My brain wouldn't focus on the words to translate them. I kept seeing the guy and the way he'd looked between me and Olive.

When we got back to the palazzo, Olive and I were held back by Corvi while Mav went to his father. We spent a fraught hour sitting on a sofa and wondering what the hell was going on.

Later, I was dragged in to Rico as well. Vin and Antonio were there, too.

Rico was pacing his study, the picture of untouchable fury.

"In my own damned house!" he was ranting, in Italian of course. "They come here, in my own house, on MY island, and threaten my future daughter-in-law? I won't stand for it!"

"What do you want us to do about it?" Vin asked.

Rico slammed his hands down on his desk and glared at the lot of us. "I want you to find the fuckers and show them how deep and bloody Vitali vengeance runs."

"I'll contact the ports and the helipad," Antonio said. "Find out who has come in and how."

Rico waved a hand dismissively. "We should have been warned already. We would have if they had any information."

"The what the fuck do you expect us to do? Use them as bait to flush these arseholes out?" Mav growled, his arms crossed over his chest.

Rico looked like he was entertaining the idea for a fraction of a second, then he shook his head. "I don't fucking care how you do it. You find them and get them off my island. You put the word out. Anyone comes near Vitali's future daughter-in-law and it's one-shot policy. I'm not taking risks. Carlione entrusted his only daughter and her friend to my care. I have a fucking duty. I made an oath. I will fuck up any man who tries to make me break that!"

"You're not the only one who made an oath," Mav reminded him.

Rico nodded to his eldest son. "No. No. Of course."

He looked at me and I smiled like I had no idea what they were talking about. As he searched me, he couldn't seem to decide if maybe he'd been mistaken about by ability to speak Italian, or maybe I was just being polite. He probably felt he knew me by now that the latter was less likely. Usually, he wouldn't have been wrong.

"How is Olive?" he asked me, switching to English.

I nodded. "As fine as she can be, I think. She just wants to know what's happening and what's going to happen. I think that's all we both want to know."

"You are both confined to the palazzo until we know more. No more sneaking off without guards. Any time you want to go outside, you will be accompanied by at least two men. Maverick will be one of them as often as possible."

"What will I do against a sniper?" Mav muttered angrily and I was going to ignore every implication of that.

"You're just going to imprison us?" I asked.

"It is for your safety, Echo." Rico was imploring me.

"We're eighteen, *Rico*," I reminded him. "We can't just stop living our lives because someone likes the look of Olive. If we did that every time, we wouldn't be here now."

"This is not the first stalker she's had?" Antonio asked.

I shook my head. "No. There was a guy from school. He was a few years ahead of us. Gave me the creeps, but she didn't see the harm in him and he took her kindness as invitation. Then there was a groundskeeper that worked for Daniel. He was a new guy. Young. Didn't try anything, he just left her presents. Weird ones, sometimes. Then one day he was gone. I've tried not to wonder if Daniel had him killed."

"This is why you think she's being stalked now?" Mav asked.

I shrugged. "I don't know much about stalkers, I know. But Olive is sweet and kind and absolutely beautiful. She has a personality that makes her literally radiant. I get the appeal."

"I think we need more evidence," Mav told his father in Italian.

I bristled. "You said you believed me. You saw him. You shot him for fuck's sake!"

"Echo, your fire is admirable," Rico said slowly. "But hear him out."

Mav glared at me, like somehow the whole thing was my fault, before looking back to his father. "I just think we need more evidence that he is stalking Olive."

"You said–" I started again, but his look of utter rage shut me up.

"We need to be sure who he is after before we launch a full-scale attack on another family. We need to know why we go to war."

"No one needs to go to war," I breathed, awestruck this was something they might go to war over. Of course, I was picturing like Pelennor Fields, rather than small skirmish, but you know.

"How else do you think we solve our problems?" Rico asked with a humourless laugh. "Treatises are tenuous at best. We are a passionate people. Hot-headed and hot blooded. We sometimes act first and ask questions later."

"Seems like a *great* way to conduct business," I muttered sarcastically.

"Why would he want Echo?" Vin asked Mav and I was going to pretend I didn't hear the condescension in his voice.

Then I blinked, not realising that was an alternative option. "Sorry, what?" I spluttered. I looked between them all. "He's… Me? No." I shook my head so violently, I made myself feel a bit ill. "I'm going to second that, Vin. Why would he want me? I'm literally nobody."

Rico pointed at me. "There. You see?" he asked Mav. "She's nobody. They want Olive. They'll use Echo as a means to get to her, but Olive is the target."

Mav looked at me and I could tell he didn't believe it. I had no idea what would make him think such a thing. But then I got that niggling feeling about the way the guy was looking at me.

"And if we are wrong?" Mav said.

Rico levelled an inquisitive look on me. "If you knew something that might save the life of anyone in this palazzo, you would tell me, no?"

I nodded. "No. I mean, yes. Of course, I would."

Rico nodded. "There," he said again, this time like it was the end of the conversation. "Echo, thank you for your time. I would have a moment with my boys."

I nodded, got up awkwardly and sidled out of the room.

On my way upstairs, my phone started ringing.

I frowned at it before answering. "Daniel?"

"Echo!" he cried. "Are you okay? Olive?"

"Did Rico contact you?" I asked.

"He told me what happened. How are you?"

I frowned harder. "Fine. Physically. Do you want to talk to her?"

"No," he said quickly. "No. That's fine. I just needed to check you were okay. Both of you."

"The Vitalis are looking after us."

"Do they know any more?"

I shook my head. "Very little. I don't know. Why don't you ask Rico?"

"He didn't so much call me to keep me abreast as called to interrogate me in case I had anything that would help them."

I nodded. "Sounds like Rico." I paused. "Why did you call *me*,

Daniel?" I asked.

"Because I trust you to take care of my Olive, Coco. And I didn't want to worry her."

I nodded again. "Okay. Well, I guess I will let you know if we know anymore."

"Sounds good. You know I'm here if you need anything."

"I do, thanks. Bye."

I hung up and finished jogging up the stairs to find Olive, wondering about the sudden weird turn our lives had taken. The week before, we were a couple of recently graduated, jet-setting best friends. Now it felt like we were at the centre of some big controversy. I didn't care for it.

CHAPTER THIRTEEN

I wasn't going to be a prisoner. I was going to make Olive stay at the palazzo to keep her safe, but she also needed *sfogliatella* – which the Americans apparently called lobster tails – and no one seemed to think it was important enough to go and do.

So, there was me, doing it.

And it wasn't like I hadn't taken precautions. I'd tucked my hair up under a giant hat and worn sunglasses. Without Olive by my side, no one was going to know I was me.

Except one person, of course.

I felt my hat yanked off my head and I turned to see Mav in all his angry glory.

"What are you doing here?" he asked me.

"I could ask you the same thing," I retorted.

"I'm doing my fucking job."

"Well, so am I."

"And what do you plan to do when they find you? Bat your eyes at them?"

I grunted at him and was not going to dignify that with an answer. "Olive needs a pick-me-up. I'm here for pastries."

"What pastries?"

"I can't pronounce them."

"Sfogliatella?"

"How did you know?"

"Famous for being hard to say." He looked around. "Fine. I will take you to get your damned pastries, then I am taking you back to the palazzo."

"Why?"

"Because there is a stalker out there and it is my oath to keep you safe."

"No, I mean, why are you letting me get the pastries."

His eyes softened as he looked at me. "You said she needed them."

I was not going to fall apart and completely and utterly lose my heart to a man who didn't dismiss my concerns for being frivolous and ridiculous, but took me seriously when I probably did look a bit frivolous and ridiculous.

We walked in silence to the shop that made Olive's favourite sfogliatella. His hand brushed against mine and I fought the urge to hold it. I didn't think Mav was the holding hands sort, let alone that a few stolen kisses and epic orgasms meant we were at the hand holding stage.

Mav and I were about two doors down from the shop when a chill ran down my spine and I froze. Ahead of me was the guy. He was looking at me the same way he'd look at me the last time. The way he'd looked between Olive and me.

I finally recognised what it was. He was confused about who we were. He was looking at the woman with Mav and not sure if she was the one he wanted. That's why he'd gone after Olive…

He'd thought she was…me.

It all slammed into place and I started backing away.

Mav had been right. The guy was after me. Little nobody me. It was irrelevant just then why he was after me. The why wasn't going to change a damn thing at that moment. The more pertinent question was what we did about it.

I felt Mav take my hand. "I will protect you," he promised.

I nodded. "No. Good. I'm sure you will."

"You don't sound sure."

"I'm scared, Mav. Give me a pass on the inability to control my vocal inflections."

"What?"

"Never mind," I grumbled, knowing the Italian word for 'inflections' as much as he clearly knew the English word. "Can't you shoot him?"

He nodded as he slowly drew a gun and trained it on the guy. "I can, but that's not going to help me find out if he's working with anyone."

"Just hand her over and this can be done with, Vitali," the guy called.

Mav dropped my hand to get a better aim on the guy. "Why don't you walk away before I send you back to your boss in a box?"

I felt hands on me and I was pulled backwards.

"Ma—" was all I got out before a hand slammed over my mouth.

I felt something cold and metallic at my temple and I felt fear the likes of which I had never felt before pierce my spine.

Mav turned and I saw the panic in his eyes. The calculation. He was weighing up the scenarios in his head and trying to work out which one got both of us out of there alive and with the information we needed. I saw the moment he realised he wasn't going to be able to do both.

"Fuck!" Mav yelled, then something was flying over my head and the guy holding me was yanked backward and something hot and wet hit me.

I was pulled with him, but his arms went slack and I scrabbled to get my footing. Mav ducked to help me, cursing like a sailor the whole damned time.

A bullet went flying past us and Mav looked up at the first guy. Whatever he saw, he reacted on lightning instinct. As the shooter pulled the trigger again, Mav spun, putting his back to the shooter, and pulled me sideways. The bullet whizzed right through where I'd stood moments before, and I felt my life flash before my eyes. It was pretty dismal, but there were two shining beacons, one of whom was standing in front of me and had just saved me from a bullet to the gut.

Then I registered the grunt of annoyance from Mav and looked down at his side. The bullet had nicked him. He looked less hurt and more pissed off as a snarl rippled over his face. Letting go of me, he pulled both his guns and whirled back to the shooter, letting rip a quick succession of four bullets. I flinched every time, but I watched as all four found their mark; three in the torso and one in the head.

It made me realise that he hadn't found his mark last time because he probably hadn't given himself the time to stop and aim properly.

"Fuck," Mav spat again, then holstered one gun, kept the other out, and took my hand.

He led me back to his car, constantly checking over his shoulder to make sure I was still there and I was okay. I felt like I was driven by pure adrenalin and fear. There was something I wanted to do, something I needed to do. I needed a minute, but I didn't know what for. I knew Mav needed to get me safe. He'd killed two of them, who knew how many more there might be?

He drove up the hill like a man possessed and the car screeched to a stop at the front door of the palazzo. He barely got the engine turned off then he was out and pulling me out my door. I had little choice but to follow him.

Rico came running, obviously curious about the noise, and saw instantly that his son what hurt.

"What happened?" he asked.

Mav started ranting as he paced back and forth. He looked about as crazy as I felt. All thoughts everywhere and body so hyped, full of restless energy it had to release. I was just too shocked to do anything about it.

"There were two of them. They nearly shot her. I had to kill them."

I had never had a doubt that Rico loved his family. In his own unique way. But the Rico before me now wasn't Lord Vitali of the crime family. He was just Mav's dad, and he recognised that his boy was going through something.

"You did," Rico agreed. "You did what you had to do to keep Echo safe."

"Now we won't know who they're working for or if there are others!" Mav was yelling.

Then Rico was yelling and Mav was yelling and I probably wouldn't have been able to understand even if they'd been speaking English. I felt like my legs were going to give way. It was like my mind was trapped inside a body it had completely lost control over.

My mind railed against the bars of a cage, while my body was ready to just give up.

I felt someone beside me and Olive was there.

"Come on," she said gently. "Let's get you cleaned up. They'll find us when they need us."

I nodded dumbly and let her lead me up the stairs, into my room, and through to the bathroom. As she turned on the shower, I caught sight of myself in the mirror. Blood splatted me, my face, my arms, my clothes. And, underneath it, I was white as a ghost. I stood, compliant, while she undressed me and got me in the shower. There was no room for prudishness between us at the best of times, I certainly didn't give a shit about her seeing me in all my glory now.

With nothing but the whispered lullaby my mum used to sing us when we were little, Olive got me clean, got me dressed again, brushed out my hair and hugged me tightly.

"I just…" I said, my voice croaky like it had been more than an hour since I'd last used it. "I just need a minute."

She searched my eyes, but seemed happy enough with what she saw there. She nodded, kissed my head, and then headed out. I went to sit on my bed, too out of it to do anything when I missed and ended up on the floor.

I didn't know how long I sat there, just picturing Mav laying waste to the guy who'd almost killed me again and again. Something about it felt cathartic, but it only served to heighten my adrenalin more.

Then, I heard familiar growled tones.

"Never fucking do that again."

I looked up and found him standing by my door. He looked

cleaned up as well, his hair still wet and his shirt whole. I watched as he closed the door and locked it behind him. I leapt to my feet as his carried him to me in a purposeful stride. He looked me over like he couldn't really believe I was standing in front of him. I kind of knew how he felt.

"Never," he repeated, "fucking do that again."

I nodded, not quite sure exactly what he meant, but agreeing with the sentiment. "I won't."

"Promise me."

I licked my lip. "Promise you what, Mav?"

He dropped his forehead to mine. "Promise me I'll never have to fear losing you like that again."

My heart pounded low and hard and slow in my chest. My beath was too shallow, too fast. My mind ran so quickly, every thought I tried to hold onto slipping out of grasp. My body was too far away from his.

I lay my hands on his chest and shook my head against his. "Never."

My hands trailed up his body as we stepped closer to each other. His hands gripped my hips firmly and warmth spread up my spine. Like we read the other's mind, our lips crashed together as our arms wound tight around each other.

Our kiss was all desperation. Fuelled by adrenalin and emotions we'd been repressing from the moment we met, we were both frantic. Our noses bumped constantly. Hands roved like they didn't know where to rest, or maybe were afraid of what they'd miss if they stopped. Like we had to make sure we were still both here and – relatively – whole and not going anywhere.

Mav's lips blazed a trail down my cheek, over my jaw, and to my neck and I took a moment to breathe. It wasn't long before his lips were claiming mine again and I knew I needed him closer.

There was this overwhelming sense of urgency, of time running out, of the fleeting finality of our mortality, and how much I would regret if I didn't touch Mav now. If he didn't touch me. I was ruled by emotion and hormones, and my mind was utterly silent on the matter. It had completely left the building. No doubts. No thoughts. Just need. Want. Feel.

I dropped my hands to the bottom of his shirt, and he helped me shuck it over his head. As our lips met again, I traced the contours of his muscles with my fingers. I wanted to know every ridge and valley by feel alone. He winced slightly as my fingers found his wound, but his eyes were clear as he looked at me.

Mav's hands went to the hem of my dress, and I felt myself smile.

"Zip," I panted against his lips, taking his hand and directing his fingers to my back.

He kissed me, slower and even more needy, as he dragged my zip down in a delicious, lingering glide. It was unnecessarily sexy, and I felt my nipples pebble against my bra. I slid my fingers into his hair and nipped his lip, telling him I was done playing slow.

I felt his crooked smirk as his hand gripped my jaw firmly and our kiss grew more frantic once more.

My hands fumbled at his jeans button, and he batted it away to take over, only breaking our kiss for as long as it took him to get the jeans undone. Then he was picking me and pressing me into the wall at my back.

With nothing by my pants and his boxer-briefs between us, his erection as it dug into me was tantalisingly close. Our bodies rocked together wantonly, both wanting more.

"Mav," I panted against his lips.

"Echo," he groaned, his tone telling me everything we would never put into words.

His fingers trailed under me and ran over my slit. I tried to grind against him. It wasn't enough. It would never be enough.

"Mav," I begged, totally caught up in everything that was him and me, and everything that could be us.

He groaned, deep and primal, then he'd slid my pants aside and I felt his tip hot and hard at my entrance. He rubbed over me, making me wetter and lubricating himself. It wasn't enough.

"Mav," I begged him again, more of a whimper really.

His eyes pinned mine and he pressed into me. Slowly at first, then in one swift plunge. I cried out softly as I my fingers dug into him and the rest of me relaxed into him. There was nothing soft and gently about our first time together. It was all carnal, pure release of emotion. All feeling, not thinking.

My orgasm came at me hard and fast, and he wasn't far behind. I felt him throb deep in me and felt a rightness I didn't know existed.

As we both fought to get our breath back, his body was the only thing holding me against the wall. We held each other tight and the relief I felt was insurmountable. It wasn't just about being alive. It was about being alive with him.

Once we were both breathing more steadily, he carried me over to the bed. We undressed each other slowly, the initial pure carnal instinct sated for now and leaving way for slightly more rational.

By the time we were both fully naked and in the bed, he was semierect again already. We lost ourselves in each other for the rest of the night. Bringing each other to heights of ecstasy and a comfort no one else could give us in that moment.

I fell asleep in his arms but, by the time I woke, he was gone.

CHAPTER FOURTEEN

Olive and I were chilling out on the patio, in lieu of anything much else to do, and Mav and Antonio were walking past.

Mav's eyes were liquid heat as he looked me over after the night before. We hadn't had time to talk about where he was when I'd woken up, but it was probably a good thing he wasn't there because Olive had knocked on the – somehow still locked from the inside – door and I'd still be sprawled butt naked on it.

"It seems to me that this is the fourth time they've been by here," Olive pointed out.

I watched them go, biting my lip at Mav's parting glance over his shoulder. "I don't know what you're implying," I informed her.

"Ugh! I'm not stupid, Coco!" Olive cried suddenly and I felt my cheeks heat.

"What do you mean?"

She sighed. "I have been waiting for you to be honest with me. And I know what you keeping silence about it means, but come on! I am your best friend. Your only friend! You can talk to me."

I cleared my throat. "What–"

"I know you and Mav are fucking."

Well, there was little point in denying it now. Guilt full-on flooded me and I actually fell to my knees in front of her. "I am so sorry," I told her, and she laughed.

"For what?"

"For being with Mav behind your back."

Olive shook her head. "I might be a little naïve about some things, Coco. But no one could miss the way you look at Mav, or realise the feeling is one hundred percent mutual."

"I hate him…" I said, but my voice was shaky, and we both knew that wasn't quite the truth anymore.

"Oh, I'm sure he hates you too with how much he can't have you properly. But that doesn't mean you shouldn't be having some epic hate sex."

"What do you know about any hate sex we may or may not be having?

She huffed a laugh. "You think I didn't know what you two were getting up to at the club? What took you so long the night after we went to the beach? You are not as subtle as you think you are, Echo Sumpter."

"And, you're really okay with it?"

She rolled her eyes and pulled me off the floor. "Of course, I am. I've only been trying to tell you since you two laid eyes on each other, and you've been resisting the whole damned time. I'm glad someone we like is making use of that body, because Lord knows that there is absolutely zero sexual tension between me and him, and less than zero chances there ever will be. Our marriage will be a sham at best. He and I both know that."

"You're not worried about how it's going to complicate things when you two do have to marry?"

She shrugged. "If my husband's going to cheat on me, then I'd want it to be with my best friend."

I appreciated the sentiment more than she knew. "I don't want to be anyone's mistress," I told her.

"Who knows how long I can draw this shit out?" she said. "Stop thinking, Coco. Go to him and hate-fuck his brains out."

I smiled at my best friends. "You think I should? Right now?"

She nodded fiercely. "Of course, I do. The next time those two go by – because you know they'll find some excuse to come back around in a few minutes – you just drag him off to the nearest cupboard for a quickie."

I smirked. "I really shouldn't just leave you–"

"You'll be leaving me with Antonio, I think that's payment enough."

Olive was right. The two of them did indeed end up coming back again very shortly after. I looked around as though worried someone else would see us, then hopped up and walked over to Mav. Antonio caught my eye and gave me a knowing smirk.

"Shut it," I warned him and he mimed locking his lips. I rolled my eyes. "Like you didn't know already, huh?"

Antonio tapped his nose. "Unlike Olive, my best friend talks to me."

I looked at Mav disapprovingly. "Seriously?"

He shrugged. "What?"

I shook my head. "Why don't you come and show me how sorry you are?" I told him, taking his hand and tugging him after me.

Humour lit Mav's eyes. "Is this what it's going to be like now?"

I nodded. "Oh, yeah. This is what it's going to be like now."

Knowing Olive knew about Mav and me, and that she was

interested in Antonio made things a little easier. The four of us were still going on 'double dates', but instead of Olive getting to know Mav, she was getting to know Antonio.

We couldn't exactly walk through the village with me and Mav holding hands, not in the least because there was still no word about the whole stalker thing. But we took to having picnics again, even if we couldn't stray as far from the palazzo as before.

Mav launched at me for a kiss and we both tumbled to the blanket. Mav rolled over me and I was lost enough in the moment to forget where we were.

"Get a room!" Olive laughed.

We didn't so much get a room as we snuck off to a very sheltered piece of vegetation. Mav made quick work of lying me down in the grass and finding his way under my skirt. He kissed me lazily as his fingers circled my clit. I wrapped my arms around his shoulders and my leg around his hip.

Moving in rhythm together, he brought me easily to orgasm. I kissed him deeper and my hands went to his waist and freed him from his trousers. I rubbed him slowly and felt him groan against me. But I needed more or him. I felt like I would always need more of him.

I directed him to my centre and he pressed into me. There was no hurry today. No pent up emotions looking for a place to explode. We had, for the most part, all the time in the world.

Mav's strokes were long and deep, rubbing against every part of me. Our arms were wrapped around each other. I was still sensitive from before, and he felt amazing.

"*Mio dio, nympha,*" he breathed reverently and I hugged him tighter.

His hand gripped my hip harder as his pace quickened. He pounded me and I could feel another orgasm building. It was just balancing on a precipice, just out of reach.

"Mav," I panted. "I'm so close…"

His hand left my hip and slid between us. As soon as his fingers brushed over my clit, my orgasm crashed into me and I arched into his body.

"Fuck," he grunted and I felt his whole body tense as he came moments later.

He thrust languidly as we kissed and rode the final waves together, then he was brushing the hair from my face and looking down at me with such tender affection in his eyes that my heart hitched in my chest.

Then he dropped his face and peppered mine with kisses. I laughed as he slid out of me quickly, tucking himself back into his pants.

"I had not planned for that to be so quick," he said.

I smiled. "Quality over quantity, baby."

He nodded, pressing one more kiss to my lips before helping me up. "Quality over quantity, little nymph."

Once we were semi-respectable once more, we headed back to the picnic blanket. When we got back, Antonio seemed to have some business to talk to Mav about. So I dropped onto the blanket and waited for them to be done.

Olive cleared her throat and I looked at her expectantly.

"Yes?"

"You and Tino…?" she started, super awkwardly.

"What about me and Tino?" I asked.

"Did… You and he…?"

I burst into laughter as I shook my head. "No. God. No. Tino and I have only ever been platonic." I paused. "Why?"

She smiled. "I would give you a taste of your own medicine and say 'nothing', but I won't."

"Proving, once again, you are the better friend."

She looked at me as though to say we both knew that wasn't true. "It's nothing major, but we kissed." She shrugged like it really was nothing.

I looked at her, waiting for more details. "What? That's it?"

Olive shrugged again. "What?"

"Just a kiss?"

"It was a very nice kiss?" she suggested.

"I mean, was it? Or are you checking to make sure?"

She rolled her eyes. "It was. It was very nice. Kind of chaste, but nothing wrong with that for a first kiss. Don't want to go all hell for leather and then be disappointed the next time out the gate."

I snorted.

"What?"

I shook my head. "No. Just. Your analogy. Plus, my first kiss with Mav was… Off the charts."

She inclined her head. "Yes, but you two are very different people than us. You're all heat and fire and ruled by your smaller heads."

"Oh, like you and Tino are earth and water, and monk-like?" I teased.

She smiled. "No! No. Not what I meant."

I nodded. "I know what you meant. As long as you thought it was perfect, then good."

"I did."

"Then, good."

"Oh, you know? I googled his little pet name for you…" Olive said slowly.

I frowned in confusion.

"Mav? *Nympha*?" she clarified, and I nodded. "It isn't just Latin for 'nymph'. It also means 'bride'."

My cheeks flamed and she was the one nodding.

"Yeah, stew on that, baby. You still want to tell me you don't know why you didn't want to tell me about him?"

I knew what she was implying. She was implying that I didn't want to tell her because I'd fallen harder for Mav than I'd let myself believe, and he'd fallen just as hard, maybe even more quickly.

"It's just lust, Ollie."

She nodded. "Sure. And I'm the queen of Sheba."

But she'd got me thinking. Not that I hadn't already been doing some of that and trying very hard to ignore it.

There was the very real possibility that I could be in love with Mav. The woman who would never be a mistress had gone and – almost – fallen in love with a man expected to propose to my best friend in a little over two months. It wouldn't matter to Lord Vitali or Lord Carlione that there was a chance Mav could love me, too. A deal was a deal, and marrying me would get the Vitalis nothing in the Carliones' circles. I was no one. The daughter of Olive's mad governess who'd had to be institutionalised and eventually succeeded in taking her own life.

It wasn't enough to make me want to end things with Mav on purpose, but it made me twitchy around him and he knew me well enough to notice instantly.

"What's wrong?" he asked me later that night in my room.

I shook my head. "Nothing. It's fine." Because it would be fine. We'd agreed we'd just live the now and not worry about the future, and I was going to stick by that.

He took my arm gently. "Echo?" he said firmly.

I sighed. "It's nothing, Mav. Okay?"

"Like us?" he asked.

I looked up at him. "Excuse me?"

"Is that it?"

"Is what it?"

"Nothing is wrong, like what it between us?"

"What does it matter what's between us, Mav?"

"Of course!" Mav cried. "It's not like it means anything. After all, I owe my life – my loyalty – to the family."

I bristled. "How could I forget? And there's absolutely no question that you might have a brain for yourself!"

"Breaking loyalties leads to war, Echo," he said, and I couldn't remember when he'd ever used my actual name before this moment. "Unrest. Instability. Loyalty to the family is all we are brought up to know."

I knew what he was saying. Sure, it wasn't in so many words, but I understood the message. Loyalty was to the family. I wasn't family. Ergo, I was pretty sure I knew how loyal he was to me.

"Far be it for the nobody to come in and shake things up. Best she do what she's good at and just provide some titillation. Daddy getting sick of your whores, Mikhail?" I sassed. "Figured he'd bring Olive in to look good on your arm, and me to look good on your cock?"

He growled. "I wouldn't expect someone not of a family to understand."

"Oh," I breathed. "Low blow, arsehole."

Confusion flickered across his face for a split second. "There are expectations on me. Expectations I will need to find a way to fulfil."

"Well, I would hate to get in the way of your little arranged marriage. You seem to have the whole thing all worked out and I looked forward to watching the two of your get more and more miserable together as the years pass."

"I'm sure it won't be half as satisfying as watching you grow old, bitter and alone," he retorted.

I felt a hot lump forming in my throat. "Then we'll all be happy."

He nodded. "We will."

He turned and headed for the door.

"Don't let your blind loyalty smack you in the arse on the way out," I warned him.

"At least I know where my loyalties lie," he threw back at me before he stormed out.

He slammed the door behind him, and I just sort of crumpled to the floor.

I had no idea what had just happened.

I hadn't intended for things to end between us, but I guess it was a two-way street, and he was playing anymore. There I was, falling in love with him and now it was over? I wasn't really sure how to feel. I worried that, if I let myself feel anything, it was going to consume me.

All I could do was remind myself that I'd known Mav for four weeks. It wasn't love. It was that obsession I'd been so worried about.

We hadn't so much been one kiss away from it, as we were in the eye and only now was it obvious what a shitstorm it was.

This was better. Now everyone could go about their ordered lives, and do exactly what was expected of them.

Yep.

This was *way* better.

CHAPTER FIFTEEN

In the wake of the thing between Mav and me blowing up, he turned his not insignificant attentions on Olive. I didn't see anything flirty or romantic, really. But he was putting in an effort to make this whole expected proposal thing be more amicable, and I felt that like the kick in the pants it was supposed to be.

And Antonio – good, sweet, agreeable, good-natured Antonio – wasn't helping any.

"Talk to him," he begged me.

I shook my head. "Don't take his side," I huffed. "I mean, I know you *have* to, but don't bring it to me. Okay? He made his feelings perfectly clear."

"That's what I'm trying–"

"Enough, Tino!" I cried. "Okay? I'm done!"

I pushed out of there and took a car down to the village. Yeah, sure, I wasn't supposed to. No one knew what was happening with the whole stalker deal. Nothing they were telling me anyway. So, as far as I knew, it was safe and fine and safe. And I was going to tell myself that as often as I needed to believe it.

I arrived early enough to still visit the market stalls, which was a rare occurrence for me. Even after almost a month here, I'd never really managed to just wander and get lost in investigating the stalls.

Olive was always distracted by the shiny things at the next stall and I enjoyed her excitement too much not to follow along with her.

So, I strolled and I pretended my life was fine.

I pretended we hadn't arrived on this island for my best friend to get to know her future husband.

I pretended I hadn't fallen that future husband.

I pretended there was no stalker who had shot that future husband instead of me.

I pretended that that future husband hadn't gone and broken my heart anyway.

And I almost believed it.

At least, I believed it enough to notice when I'd been noticed. And not in a bad way.

There was a *very* hot guy watching me from the other side of the market aisle. I'd caught him looking out the corner of my eye. I turned to him, and a bright, sexy smile blossomed across his face as he looked away just late enough that I knew he was teasing me.

His hair was longer than Mav's – not that Maverick Vitali was the bar by which all men must be measured – and it was a little lighter, curlier. His skin was more tanned, like he spent a lot of time outside. He wore a thing white cotton shirt with the sleeves rolled up, and light khaki shorts that fell to his knees. He was wearing something like a loafer or espadrille, again with the no socks. I didn't let that put me off.

And he wanted me to know he was looking – perchance even that he was interested – but was letting me do with that what I would. What I wanted to do with it was probably not very advisable after the recent we-weren't-even-dating-so-it-wasn't-even-a-break-up fiasco.

Very obviously pretending that I wasn't watching him, I sauntered over to the other side of the aisle, making for the next stall up. Matching my pace, he also made for the next stall. Keeping one eye on him beside me, I fingered the offerings at the stall. They were trinkets really – the market being filled with things to appeal specifically to tourists over the Summer months – like jewellery and coin purses and keyrings. All handmade. Intricate. Gorgeous. I'd been eyeing things off at this stall all Summer.

Coincidentally, although I suspected totally on purpose, his hand reached for a necklace at the same time as me and our fingers brushed. I got a little zing from it and felt myself bite my lip as I looked at him through my eyelashes. I gently and slowly slid my hand back and let him pick it up. It was a Murano glass heart in a gorgeous brown and green swirling pattern, fastened on a thin, brown leather cord.

His grin was wide and sincere. "This one matches your eyes," he said in flawless Italian.

I smiled. "Thank you," I replied in English.

"On holiday?" he asked, switching to English as well.

Did he really not know who I was?

Well, no, of course not. No one who knew who I was would have approached me like this. They hadn't in the last month, why would they suddenly start now?

I nodded. "Uh, yes. You?"

He inclined his head as he looked over the stall offerings again. "*Si*. Yes."

"Alone?" actually popped out of me like I was the most desperate, deprived person on the planet.

I know I was trying to pretend that Mav didn't exist and a great way to do that would be to just leap into bed with this very handsome stranger. But, as much as that was my default setting, there was something holding me back from getting carried away with it.

"I am. You speak English, but don't sound British. Puts you a long way from home to be alone."

"Then it's a good thing I'm not."

"Ah." He nodded. "Boyfriend?"

The laugh that escaped me was more like a coquettish giggle and I was disgusted. I was not that girl. Power to those that were, but that wasn't me. I cleared my throat, making myself look even more guilty and awkward. It was like, the harder I was trying *not* to flirt with him, the more I sounded like I was.

"No," I told him. "Just friend. She's…back at the hotel." Close enough.

"*Bene*." He held a hand out to me. "Enzo."

I gave him my hand. "Echo."

His warm, easy grin widened. "Similar, no?"

I nodded. "They are."

He turned to the stall owner, who I'm sure was rolling their eyes over the umpteenth couple they'd seen flirting at market stalls, and bought the necklace.

"*Grazie*," Enzo said with a nod, then held the necklace to me. "For you."

"Thank you, but I can't accept that."

"I meant it only as a good gesture."

I smiled. "No. I mean, it's far too expensive for a gift for someone you don't know."

He looked around like he was thinking 'yes, I suppose so, what a shame,' then back to me like he had an answer. "Then why don't we eat and get to know each other. I will even let you pay for yourself. Just two people sharing a table. Nothing more."

The idea was almost too appealing to pass up. No strings. Just sharing good food and the time with someone else in this world. We could go our separate ways and let that be the end of it.

"Why not?" I said warmly.

"Any suggestions?" he asked.

I nodded. I had a great suggestion actually. "Yes. Follow me."

"So, tell me about you," I said as we sat down.

"Me?" he said, blowing out sharply. "Well, I studied a degree in business and economics so I was properly prepared to take on my father's enterprise. We then had a falling out and I decided to travel the world."

I nodded sympathetically. "He cut you off?"

He huffed a rough laugh. "Oddly, no. His anger manifested in an order to 'go and find myself'. He said whoever I was now was a useless idiot and he couldn't stand to look at me anymore."

I gasped teasingly. "What if you come back worse?"

His smile was pure gold, making the corners of his eyes crinkle. "Why do you think I am still travelling?"

I leant my chin on my hand as I looked at him. "That sounds nice."

"You want to travel?"

I shrugged. "I mean, I'm literally *on* holiday right now. I can't really complain I've not travelled."

"And yet?" he guessed.

"And yet, I don't feel like I'm travelling?" It came out a question, because I wasn't quite sure what I meant by that.

"What do you feel like? What do you want to do with your life?"

"Okay, in an ideal world, I'd study history and make my way up to a PhD so I could get grants and travel all over to investigate castles and records and burial sites. I would do nothing except learn and be beholden to no one."

He was smart enough to know where I was going with that. "But it's not an ideal world."

"No, it's not."

"And so, what will you do?"

"I will do a degree in language and culture so I can travel with my friend in ease and comfort, able to translate for her reliably and comfortably, making us reliant on no one."

"You care a lot for her, this friend?"

I nodded. "She's my world. Even in that ideal world, I'm not sure I could ever really leave her behind. I want to be with her more than I want my own life." I laughed at the sudden brevity the conversation had fallen under. "Sorry, that got kind of heavy. Uh, I also like punk rock, sleeping in, and really thick eyeliner."

He laughed, deep and warm, and it was a sound that made me smile. "Good to know."

There was undeniably a connection there. It was flickering to life between us as we sat and ate and chatted. I hadn't felt that carefree since we'd first arrived on the island. Before Mav and the stalker and everything else. It made me think of simpler times when I could really envision being essentially stuck here for the rest of my life.

Enzo and I sat there for too long, really. It was close to five when I was finally pulling into the palazzo garage and hurrying back inside.

"Um, excuse me," Olive said when she saw me.

I grinned at her. "Excuse you?"

She nodded. "You look ridiculously happy."

I shrugged. "I had a good day."

"Did you talk to Mav?" she asked and all happiness dropped. "I guess not. Did you meet someone?"

I tried very hard not to smile widely at her question. "No."

"You so did," she accused.

"If you mean in the literal sense, do I now have the acquaintance of someone I didn't this morning, then yes, I 'met someone'. If you however meant did I strike up a flirtation with a *very* sexy member humanity, then no."

"I mean, literally no one believes you, but okay," she laughed. "What's his name?"

I considered pretending not to know who she was talking about. But then I figured I couldn't very well talk about him if I didn't admit he existed. "Enzo."

"*Trés chic.*"

I snorted. "Wrong language."

She flapped her hands in a 'whatever' gesture. "It's a global phrase."

I rolled my eyes as I headed up to my room. "Whatever. I need to change."

"Why? Because you smell like sexy foreign man and can't possibly be caught *in flagrante*?"

"Now you speak Latin?" I teased. "And are legally trained?"

She huffed, but it was good-natured frustration. "Yes, yes. Echo's all obsessed with words and language and knows what stuff means."

I snorted. "It still sounds dirty."

Her nose scrunched adorably. "Isn't it?"

I shook my head. "It just means doing something wrong. Fancy Latin for 'caught red handed', basically."

"That is far less funny than being caught giving a blow job."

I nodded and pointed at her. "You are not wrong."

I was buoyed enough by the events of the day that even Mav studiously ignoring me from the other side of the table couldn't dampen my mood. I actually found myself humming. I hadn't hummed in…quite possibly years. Not around other humans anyway.

"I didn't realise you were musical, Echo," Rico said.

I looked up quickly. "Uh, I'm not."

Olive snorted. "She was choir leader at school."

I scrunched my nose. "It's not a glamorous as it sounds."

"Sing us a song after dinner," Rico said. "We shall judge how…glamorous it is."

So, I was stuck spending the rest of the dinner trying to come up with a song to sing for them after. My eyes accidentally rose to Mav and I couldn't shake the idea of one specific song I loved. I nodded to myself and readied myself to sing it.

Maisy Kay's 'Almost Touch Me'.

I'd spent months perfecting it for a talent show at school with the intention of shocking all the nuns out of their habits. It wasn't a perfect rendition; it was a slower more ballad-style arrangement. It was though perfect for the way I thought about Mav. Maybe it could serve as both a bit of payback as well as closure.

As so often with Mav, I couldn't get a read on his reaction. He was as cold and haughty as ever, looking more bored than anything else. But he sat through the four more songs that Rico requested before declaring that an old man had to go to bed.

"Good night," was the only excuse we got from Mav for leaving, and Vin followed him out.

"Do you get the feeling Vin doesn't like us very much?" I asked Olive.

"You currently think none of the Vitalis like you."

I nodded. "I'm quite sure they don't. The stalker doesn't want you, do they? No. They want the little trouble-making best friend who everyone wished had stayed at home."

Olive took my arm as she led me up to our rooms. "I don't wish you'd stayed home."

I leant against her with a smile. "No. I know."

And I did, but it didn't make it any easier to stomach the idea that all the shit things that were currently happening were all my fault.

CHAPTER SIXTEEN

Olive stormed into my room later that night and frowned at me.

"What?" I asked her.

"I love you, Coco, but you are infuriating!" Olive hissed and I blinked.

"Excuse me?"

"No!" she huffed. "No. No more excusing you, madam."

"Madam?" I asked incredulously. "You're going to madam me?"

Olive nodded. "I'm going to madam you. Just watch out or I'll ground you as well."

"Where is this even coming from?" I asked.

"From your stupidity!"

"My–"

"Don't interrupt me!" she snapped and I had never loved this woman more.

With her finger pointing at me and the utter fury on her face, this was an Olive I'd never seen before in my life. She wasn't just assertive, she was commanding. She was fierce and not someone who was going to sit idly by while someone else decided their destiny for them. Like a goddess, ready to burn the world just because she could and she was sick of everyone's shit.

"You are always getting in your own damned way. You and Mav

are… Jesus, Coco. I don't think anyone could ever look at me the way he looks at you–"

"Ollie," I chastised.

She shook her head. "No. Not because I'm not worth it. I just don't think there's any love story in the whole real world like the one you two could have if you just GOT OUT OF YOUR OWN FUCKING WAY!" She yelled at me in anger, then stormed out of the room.

I was left feeling like nothing short of a slow clap was appropriate. And wondering what in the hell had happened since I saw her last to elicit that kind of tirade from her.

As a message, it had been short, sharp, and rather inelegant. But I'd received it.

Olive was right. Of course, she was. She usually was.

Finding Mav and getting out of my own damned way took me a little longer to admit was necessary. The fight we'd had was ridiculous. I couldn't even rightly remember what either of us had actually said. Had we insulted each other or just been flustered? Had it meant anything or just been a weird lack of communication?

I opened my bedroom door to go and find him only to find him standing there.

His expression was the same one I felt on my face; hesitant warmth hiding behind an uncertainty for how he'd be received. I wondered if my dear best friend had gone and yelled at him, as well.

"I'm sorry," we both said at the same time, then both tried to fight the awkward humour.

I pointed at him to indicate he go first.

He took a breath. "That fight was…" He sighed.

"Stupid?" I suggested as I invited him in.

He nodded as he took enough steps into the room to let me close the door. "*Si*. Stupid. I said some things I did not… Things I didn't mean. I want to say I don't know where they came from, but I do. I can admit when I'm wrong and I can admit that I was scared, little nymph. Scared that this foreign little woman had unlocked emotions and feelings in me I didn't know existed. That I didn't know people like me could feel, much less enjoy. Scared that she was going to unlock them and then break me. I overreacted to what I think was your fear."

I took a breath. The truth was going to be weird and awkward to admit, but it had to be done if I wanted to explore an actual grown-up, long-term relationship with anyone, especially Mav.

So, I told him, "Yes. I was scared, too. It was fine when it was just lust. Then it obviously wasn't. I'm not sure exactly what it is, or what it could be, what the future holds, but I want to find out. I want to give us time and space to see where this could go. You're my first—"

He smirked. "I know you are not talking about sex."

I bit my lip against a smile. "No. Not sex. Feelings. I've never met a guy I want to spend more time than a few hours with. Let alone a guy I want to talk to. Go to dinner with. Argue with. Sit in total, comfortable silence and watch a movie with. But you're supposed to propose to my best friend in two months and it terrified me that I was falling for you – hard – and, the harder I fell, the more fucked up it was going to be later."

He nodded like he understood. "And now?"

"Now, I dunno. Even when you and Olive marry, it seems like no one's worried you might actually be anything more than friends, so maybe it won't be so weird. Then again, there's another two months before you're supposed to propose, who knows what's going to happen by then? And I mean, who knows how long Ollie will be able to drag out the wedding, and–"

Mav shut me up with a heated kiss and I felt myself relax. He pulled away to look at me with a deep desire in his eyes, but also something smouldering away that could very possibly ignite into real love one day.

"Breathe," he said softly, a smile playing at his lips.

"Breathe," I repeated because, faced with a smile like that, I definitely needed reminding.

"What do you want to do, *nympha*?"

"I want to know what this is between us," I told him.

"I don't know what's between us, but I care about you, Echo. You are all I can think about. You're the only thing I want. Everything I am is so wrapped up in you, I feel like I've lost my mind. The way you make me feel, I don't want to find it again. All I know is you, and I just know you feel the same, no matter how much I try to tell myself that's impossible."

I did feel the same. And I knew what he meant about the knowing it. Since the day we'd met, I'd had this unshakable knowledge that he'd been as into and affected by me as I'd been by him. I'd also tried telling myself I couldn't know that, that I couldn't be right, because I couldn't read his mind. And still, I felt it in my soul. At the confirmation I wasn't the only one, I stopped pretending to resist it and realised it for what it was; a connection the likes of which I'd never felt before.

"I want us to have a chance, Mav."

"Then give us a chance," he begged me, his lips brushing against mine.

I beathed in deeply but, before I could open my mouth, he put his finger on it.

"As you said, two months is a long time. Let us enjoy the now. We have time to worry about the future later."

I nodded. "I was just going to ask you if you were planning on staying?"

His eyebrow quirked and that headted desire pooled in his eyes. "Are you asking me to stay?"

"I think you know the answer to that question, Mav. But, I will be over here, on my bed, naked, if you were thinking maybe you wanted to do something about that."

I started backing over to the bed. Mav growled playfully, lunged and swept me into his arms and we fell onto the bed together.

My phone buzzed all night, but I could tell from my watch that it was just Olive bugging me about whether we'd made up or not. Finally, I sent her a reply to say we had, and she voluntarily decided to give us some space for some alone time.

"You two are codependant?" Mav said, again like he wasn't sure he was using the right word when he knew full well that he was.

I smirked at him. "Pot meet kettle."

He nodded. "*Si.*" He wrapped me in his arms and trailed kissed over my body. "How about dinner tomorrow night?" he asked.

I nodded, pretending to think about it. "I like dinner. Night time is a good time to have it. And I'm fond of it being a daily occurrence."

He chuckled. "You know what I meant."

I shrugged cheekily. "I mean, do I?"

He took a deep breath like he was praying for patience. "Would you have dinner with me tomorrow?" he asked. "I thought to take you out for a redo of our first dinner, but I don't think my father will let you out of the palazzo."

"Our first dinner?" was the thing I latched onto.

"I also don't know where I can get any walls at such short notice."

I shoved him playfully. "Ha ha. You're so funny."

He grinned at me and it was all sexy. "I am."

That night, I fell asleep in his arms again but, when I woke up, he was still there. Albeit on his way out.

"I didn't mean to wake you."

I shook my head. "You didn't. I don't think. You're leaving?"

He nodded and leant over to give me a kiss. "Business."

I smirked. "Business," I mimicked his sombre tone whenever he said it. "Sounds fun. Don't get too much blood on your clothes."

"Why do you think I wear so much black?" he asked as he stood up.

I used his absence to stretched across the bed. "I assumed it was a dramatic fashion choice."

He inclined his head. "Perhaps there were two reasons."

I lauged and threw a pillow at him. "Go. Get to your business. The sooner you go, the sooner you can come back."

"Dinner," he promised.

I nodded. "Dinner."

Soon after he left, Olive arrived, having been haning out waiting for him to leace. Naturally, she needed a complete rundown of the night before. And she made me repeat it to her numerous times until she was needed for something after lunch with Adriana.

Whie she was occupied and Mav was on business, I thought it would be good to get out and go for a walk. I'd been cooped up too long. I could just be quick. Pop down the hill a bit, have a ramble, and come straight back in time for dinner with Mav. Easy.

Less easy. I got distracted, and went further than I meant to. Once I was heading back to the car, I dug my phone out of my pocket and thought I'd call Mav to give him a head's up so he didn't freak out.

The call went straight to voicemail and, while I listened to the recorded message do its thing, I practised what I'd say. With the car in sight, I started to leave my message.

And that was when the shit decided to hit the fan.

I felt the hairs at the back of my neck prickle.

That wasn't a good sign.

With my phone still to my ear, I fought the urge to turn around and look for whoever was causing it.

If I could just get back to the car, then–

CHAPTER SEVENTEEN: MAV

"Get it done," I told them before hanging up the phone and checking what all the notifications had been about.

There was a missed call and a voicemail from Echo. The voicemail had come through an hour earlier. The nothing. That was weird. She didn't usually call me. In fact, I couldn't remember a time she had. It had only been a few weeks, but it still sent alarm bells clanging in my chest.

I dialled the number to listen to it.

"Hi," came her bright clear voice.

Nothing sounded wrong. I couldn't hear much of anything going on in the background and pictured her sitting in her room. Had she called me just to say hello?

"Everything's fine. I'm just running a little late. I ducked out for a ramble. I know you're going to say it was a risk I shouldn't have taken. But honestly, who else is going to be out here?"

I both loved and hated that she knew me well enough to know exactly how I'd react and that she was, before even seeing me, trying to soothe me.

"I'm just heading back to the car so, I should be maybe twenty minutes away? Then I'll come find you. I don't care if you're in the middle of a murdering, I need a kiss."

My heart thudded in my chest, and it hurt so bad it burned. It took me a second to work out why. Then I realised what she'd said, and I missed her next words.

Twenty minutes.

That was an hour ago.

Then another sound brought me back to the voicemail.

It was the unmistakable sound of an explosion. The phone clattered and there was nothing more from Echo. I heard footsteps.

"Is it Mariana?" a gruff voice asked.

"It's her."

"Who was she calling?"

"Who cares. We finally have her. Smash the phone and we'll call our ride."

The call broke off, but I was frozen. My heart felt like it had stopped. Something ugly was trying to claw it's way up my throat. My fingers itched to close around someone's neck and watch as the life left their eyes. I wanted to empty my clip into their body and watch, with glee, as they bled out.

A roar of anguish left me, and I leant on my desk. "Fucking arseholes."

I grabbed the earpiece from my top draw and my other gun. I rarely conducted business without one and a knife, but this job felt like it required more firepower.

Feasibly, they might not have left the island yet. If they'd grabbed her by luck rather than planning and had to get their ride organised, then it was possible that ride would take a couple of hours to be ready for them. I would plan an assault on the whole damned island if it got her back.

The first person I had to talk to would be my father. I barged into my father's study and every pair of eyes in there looked up at me in surprise.

"Maverick, this is unprecedented," he said. "Had you wanted to be part of this meeting, you could have just told me."

I snarled. "Fuck your meeting, old man. The stalker we thought was after Olive?"

Dad sat up straighter, all attempts a joviality aside. "Yes?"

"They came for Echo."

Everyone knew that, on paper, Olive was the more important person of the two of them. More important to keep happy, to keep safe, to be friendly with. Everyone also knew that Echo and her fucking abrasive, sarcastic, no-nonsense attitude had won more than just my heart in the month the two young women had been with us. My father might have had an eye for Olive, but his mind was better matched by Echo and that counted for a lot in his book.

"Who was it?"

"I don't know."

Dad stood up. "OUT!" he cried at the others and they left as quickly as possible. "Where is she?"

"I don't know." My voice was starting to take on a slightly hysterical, wavery angry tone to it as each of his questions made me feel more and more useless. "She left me a voice message an hour ago. It cut off, but whoever had her said they needed to call their ride."

Dad came to the same conclusion as me. "She may still be on the island. I will call the locals, tell them to shut down the ferry."

I inclined my head. "I will take my bike. Send the men out. She must be found."

"She will be found, son." There was a note of sympathy in his voice that I needed to crush.

I inclined my head. "Olive will never forgive us if we lose her."

Dad inclined his head as well. "Of course. For Olive."

I frowned as I remembered something from the voicemail. "Who is Mariana?"

Dad blinked. "What?"

"Mariana. Whoever has her seemed to be calling her Mariana."

I'd never seen my father overly worried in my whole life. I don't think I'd ever seen him scared. But, as I watched, the blood drained from his face and he held out a shaky hand. "Give me your phone, cub…"

It had been many years since my father referred to me by any kind of term of affection or endearment, so I knew that the situation was serious. I dug my phone out of my pocket and passed it to him quickly, unlocking it as I did.

He found the voicemail and I saw the concern on his face. "No," he whispered more to himself. "It cannot be."

Only once he'd handed my phone back to me did I ask, "What is it?"

He shook his head. "I'd heard rumours, but… No. It couldn't be. Coincidence. That's all." He forced a smile for me. "Come. Tell Olive the news, then go."

I knew when I was being dismissed, and I was itching to get out there, so I had no interest in staying anyway. I gave him a single nod and hurried out. As I left, I saw him picking up his phone. Part of me was interested in what he was in such a hurry to do. The part of me desperate to find Echo didn't give a single shit.

I hurried up to Olive's room, sticking the earpiece in as I went. I'd need to get Antonio ready, but dad was right; Olive needed to know what we did.

"Mav, what is it?" she asked, her smile falling as she took in my face.

"They came for Echo," I told her and I saw she understood what I was saying.

She stumbled back. "What?"

I could only take a step towards her and be ready to catch her if she crumpled. "They have her. I will get her back," I promised her and realised there was perhaps too much in my voice.

"Your father still expects us to get engaged at the end of the summer," she said slowly, her unfocussed eyes finally locking onto mine.

I nodded. "Yes, and I will honour the promise made by our fathers no matter what happens. That includes keeping both of you safe."

She shook her head sadly. "But you don't want to."

Did she still think that little of me? I wouldn't blame her. "I would give my life for both of you."

"No." Her head shake was quicker this time. "No. Get engaged to me, I mean."

I looked up at her with a frown, wondering what that had to do with getting Echo back now. "Neither do you."

"No. I think it's time we had a frank discussion, here, Mav."

Seriously? "Now?"

"Yes. It won't take long, and I think it's a good time."

It was a testament to the fact that we'd started to become friends in the last week that I would entertain her for a minute or two. "What are you talking about?"

"I'm talking about what we're going to do with the fact you're in love with my best friend and, in the spirit of being honest, I'm more interested in Antonio than I ever will be in you."

I smirked, despite all the other shit going down. "You and Tino?"

She shrugged. "Well, no. I mean, maybe. Nothing yet. Not really. But I think there's a chance."

I could only nod. The few times I hadn't been stuck up my own arse, or losing my mind over Echo, I'd wondered if there was something between them. I just hadn't known that my wallflower of an intended bride had it in her. But then, I should have known because it wasn't the first time she was showing me this side of her.

"So," she continued pointedly. "I guess I'm asking you what you plan to do about it?"

There were so many things that needed seeing to just then. "About what?"

"About your feelings for Coco."

"I need to save her."

She rolled her eyes as only Olive Carlione could. "After that, Mav."

I grunted, hating these two woman and their audacity to demand things of me and, equally, my inability to deny them. "I would marry *her* if I could, Olive."

She fixed me with those big, blue eyes, and I could see what

Antonio saw in her. There was a fierceness to her I wished she'd shown when she first arrived, then maybe I wouldn't have fallen for Echo, and we'd be in less mess.

"Then get her back and do it."

"She might not have me."

Olive scoffed. "Oh, she'll *have* you. She just might not *marry* you. Yet."

I spared her a small smile, nodded my head, then hurried out.

It was irrelevant whether Echo would have me or marry me if I couldn't find her and bring her back. To even think of her needing saving would ensure she smacked me when I saw her next. I knew how strong and capable she was, even if I wanted to pretend I didn't so she'd get annoyed with me and sass the shit out of me. However, the fact seeing her next was a serious 'if' at that point, I'd gladly take the hit because it would mean I succeeded.

"Tino," I barked into my phone when he picked up.

"Boss?"

"We're going for a ride."

"On my way."

A few minutes later, I heard his voice over the earpiece and knew the others joining the search were coming online as well. It would be easier for all of us if we could talk relatively hands-free.

Antonio had perhaps more reasons than me for wanting to bring Echo back, given I assumed he was more interested in making Olive happy than I was. I wanted Olive to be happy – and I would kill or be killed to make it happen – but Echo and only Echo was my priority.

I'd just been able to call her mine, say I was hers, and I wasn't about to let anyone come between me and my little nymph. My father had named me as a reminder of a family vendetta. Whoever had my woman was about to feel just how seriously the Vitalis took their vendettas.

LITTLE SECRET

An island paradise, the other guy, and the deadly secret that could ruin it all.

Discover who wants a nobody like Echo and why they'll stop at nothing to keep her. With betrayals, and loyalties tested, Echo will have to rediscover who she can trust to get her back to Olive in one piece.

Out April 2024. Get it here: https://books2read.com/u/3k2M8L.

LITTLE NYMPH SERIES

If you liked *Little Nymph*, share the love and let me know! Echo and Mav's story crosses a trilogy, and there won't be a proper resolution until the end of book three. Major cliff-hangers like this are a new experiment for me, so hopefully they work out okay.

April 2023 · April 2024 · April 2025

REIGN

If you liked *Little Nymph*, you might also enjoy *Reign*. A New Adult darker, high school, bully romance. Get it here: https://books2read.com/u/4D6Qa7

From Elizabeth Stevens, writing as E.J. Knox, comes…

A King. An Heir. And the unwilling pawn with the power to win or crush a Royal coup.

Beckett Maxwell reigns over Rivermont Academy with his loyal court: the Royals, their courtiers, their harem. He doesn't have time for a nobody like me: a scholarship student and daughter of faculty to boot. I'm the lowest of the low in a school full of highs.

One year everything's going fine. Enough. The next, I'm some pawn in a Royal power struggle. Well, I won't have it. They can bully me, they can torment me, they can make my life miserable. But I will not be used in one of their twisted games.

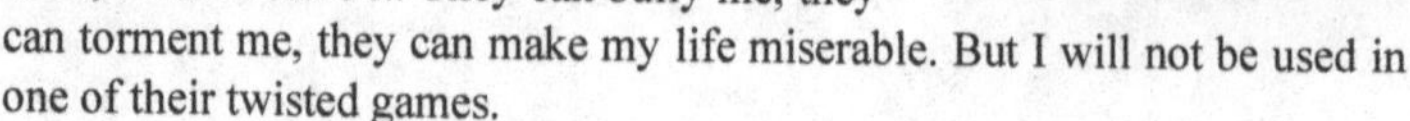

But when the fox is lurking at the door, sometimes the only safety is in the arms of the lion. Beckett might actually be the lesser evil in this case. And I can't deny there's something between us. Something I wish wasn't there.

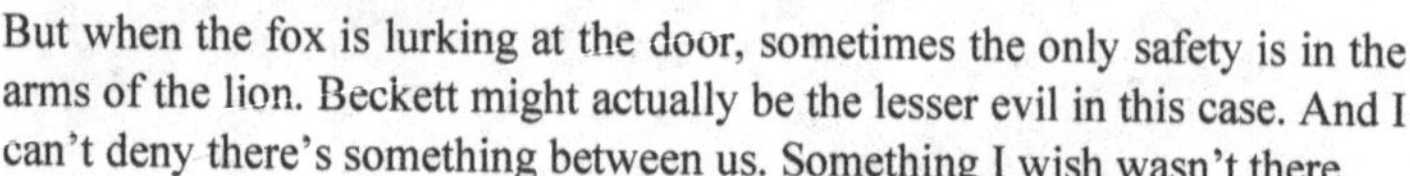

The closer we get, the further he pushes me away, but something keeps pulling me back. When it comes to Beckett Maxwell, I'm a sucker for punishment.

But I'll only bear it so long. If Beckett wants his claim on me to stick, then he might need to choose between his crown and my heart..

GODS & ANGELS

If you liked *Little Nymph*, you might also enjoy *Gods & Angels*. A New Adult darker, high school, bully romance. Book 3 is coming soon! Get it here: https://books2read.com/u/38yaGw

From Elizabeth Stevens, writing as E.J. Knox, comes…

A ruthless god. A sinful angel. And the princess between them.

My life is perfect. My life is planned. My life isn't mine.
Promised to a man I love. A man I hate. Not even a man. A god.
Apollo Callahan is that and much more.

My life is broken. My life is fractured. My life isn't free.
Craving a man I hate. A man I need. Not even a man. An angel.
Valen Kincaid is nothing I could ever want.

Though the Saints rule the hallowed halls of Saint Benedict's College, they're anything but saintly. Behind closed doors, they call themselves the Sinners. Sex. Fast Cars. Drugs. Money. The odd assassination or two. Nothing is beneath them, except the next in a long line of women. Can one little princess, searching to break free from her prison tower, bring these mighty lords crashing to their knees?

The stunning first book in the Sinners of Saint Benedicts series.

PRINCE OF THORNS

If you liked *Little Nymph*, you might also enjoy *Prince of Thorns*. A New Adult darker, enemies-to-lovers, academy, gang romance. Get it here: https://books2read.com/u/bryaD7

From Elizabeth Stevens, writing as E.J. Knox, comes…

The bad boy willing to risk everything – even his life – to get the girl.

People call them the V.I.C.E.S. because they'll wring you for everything you are and leave you ruined. They are the Princes of Rosewood Hall, and no one says no to them. Until now.

Vaughn Saint. The racer. He dubbed the Prince of Thorns. Pretty as a rose, but one touch and he'll leave you bleeding.

He chases death on two wheels at least twice a week. Used to controlling powerful things between his thighs, nothing is more powerful than the lure of the pleasures he promises.

And he wants to give them all to me. Only problem? I'm the daughter of the leader of the Blood Roses. His leader. I'm off-limits. Dad wants me to walk away from all that, not get dragged down deeper into their hell, but Vaughn Saint threatens to take me to the very depths and still have me begging for more. Loving me will kill him.

Not loving me will destroy the both of us.

LITTLE NYMPH

Thank you so much for reading this story! Word of mouth is super valuable to authors. So, if you have a few moments to rate/review Echo and Mav's story – or, even just pass it on to a friend – I would be really appreciative.

Have you looked for my books in store, or at your local or school library and can't find them? Just let your friendly staff member or librarian know that they can order copies directly from LightningSource/Ingram.

If you want to keep up to date with my new releases, rambles and writing progress, sign up to my newsletter at https://landing.mailerlite.com/webforms/landing/y1n6q2.

You can find the playlist for Little Nymph on Spotify:
I also have a generic writing playlist you can check out 😊

Follow me:

THANKS

So, *scratches head*, this book is not at all what I envisioned when I first got the idea. I wanted to go dark and suspenseful and all kinds of delicious dirtiness. Then Echo came along and Miss Sassy-Britches herself just kind of took over. I'm not mad, by any means, I'm just…left hankering for another story idea that might achieve my original goal lol.

Less thanks, and more apology to Julie. I still think about you every time I write the word 'it'. I felt like there were A LOT in this one, so…my bad.

MY BOOKS

E.J.'s list is firing up. While you wait for the next release, you can find where to buy all my books in print and eBook at the website; www.elizabethstevens.com.au/ej-knox.

ABOUT THE AUTHOR

E.J. Knox is the Darker/Bully Romance penname of Elizabeth Stevens. E.J. is the name to read if you want darker/bully romance in the Mature YA/NA crossover space. Think high school, college, and academy. E.J. brings my usual wit, banter, and repartee in good old enemies-to-lovers showdowns between alpha males and the sassy heroines strong enough to knock them down a peg or two. There'll be fake-dating, love triangles, kidnapping and danger, second chances, and more.

Writer. Reader. Perpetual student. Nerd.

Born in New Zealand to a Brit and an Australian, I am a writer with a passion for all things storytelling. I love reading, writing, TV and movies, gaming, and spending time with family and friends. I am an avid fan of British comedy, superheroes, and SuperWhoLock. I have too many favourite books, but I fell in love with reading after Isobelle Carmody's *Obernewtyn*. I am obsessed with all things mythological – my current focus being old-style Irish faeries. I live in Adelaide (South Australia) with my long-suffering husband, delirious dog, mad cat, two chickens, and a lazy turtle.

Contact me:
Email: ejknox@elizabethstevens.com.au
Website: www.elizabethstevens.com.au/ej-knox
Twitter: www.twitter.com/writer_iz
Instagram: www.instagram.com/writeriz
Facebook: https://www.facebook.com/elizabethstevens88/